SHERIFF OF MAD RIVER

The fatality rate for lawmen in Mad River was fairly high. In addition, Tim Parker was hoping that he was going to be able to hang up his guns and no longer rely on trigger law. But the call of duty proved stronger than the attractions of personal comfort.

SHERIFF OF MAD RIVER

Dan Roberts

ATLANTIC LARGE PRINT
Chivers Press, Bath, England.
John Curley & Associates Inc.,
South Yarmouth, Mass., USA.

Fic
ROB
Large
Print

Library of Congress Cataloging in Publication Data

Roberts, Dan.
    Sheriff of Mad River.
    Reprint. Originally published: New York : Lenox
Hill, 1970.
    1. Large type books.   I. Title.
(PS3568.O2378S54 1988]   813'.54   88–3582
ISBN 1–55504–594–4

British Library Cataloguing in Publication Data

Roberts, Dan, *1912–*
    Sheriff of Mad River.
    Rn: W.E.D. Ross   I. Title
    813'.54[F]

ISBN 0–7451–9374–9

This Large Print edition is published by Chivers Press, England, and
John Curley & Associates, Inc, U.S.A. 1988

Published by arrangement with Donald MacCampbell, Inc

U.K. Hardback ISBN 0 7451 9374 9
U.S.A. Softback ISBN 1 55504 594 4

SHERIFF OF MAD RIVER

CHAPTER ONE

The road to Mad River, Wyoming, was rough and dusty. And on this cool starry night, the stage was crowded, which didn't tend to make it any more comfortable. They had made their last stop before arriving at Mad River, and because of a troublesome shoe on one of the horses, they had been forced to lose some time at a livery stable in the small town. Now they would arrive in Mad River late.

'Might as well take it as it comes,' the driver had warned his five passengers. 'We ain't going to see the end of this trip until after midnight.'

Tim Parker sat ramrod straight against the lurching of the stage and observed the others in the vehicle with him rather disdainfully. He had left Ohio to take on an assignment in Mad River. This was no new experience for him. For quite a while now he'd been on the move from town to town throughout the West, selling his gun to the highest bidder. And he didn't care whether the highest bidder was on the right side of the law or the wrong one.

He didn't look the hard-bitten gunman type. True, he had a stern expression most of the time, but his face was even-featured and pleasant. He was bronzed from years in the

1

saddle, and his corn-yellow hair and pale blue eyes stood out against the dark color of his skin.

In Mad River he was reporting to a man named Jim Trent, who owned the town's largest hardware store as well as a half-dozen ranches. Trent had heard about him and sent word he could use a man handy with a Colt .44 and would pay well. The message had come at just the right time. Tim had wound up his work in Ohio and was looking for something else. Mad River offered something else.

The stage hit an extra bad bump, and the old man sitting next to Tim lurched hard against him, spilling some whiskey from the open bottle he was holding in his hand over both himself and Tim. As they recovered from the incident, the old man offered Tim a toothless smile.

'Sorry, young fella,' he said. 'I didn't intend to sprinkle you with my special brand of firewater.' He was a wizened old gent with a mangy black beard, and he had the common name of Sam Smith. But he was an uncommon character. Some time back he'd hit it rich in gold, and after years as a lonely prospector he was a millionaire. He'd built himself a castle outside Mad River and lived in it alone except for a half-dozen Sioux servants. His clothes were a shabby black, and his mangy brown Stetson had seen better

2

days. Despite his wealth, he still looked and acted like the poor prospector he'd been.

Tim Parker gave him an easy smile. 'No harm done,' he said. He had put the old man down as a genial, harmless crank who enjoyed talking almost as much as he did whiskey.

'Man gets thirsty on a trip like this,' Sam Smith said, lifting the bottle to take a snort. When he put it down and smacked his lips, he offered a friendly grin to a reserved, gray-haired man seated opposite him, with a pretty blonde girl in a brown cape and bonnet at his side. This duo were Preacher Abel Gray and his daughter, Sabrina. The preacher was hoping to establish a church in Mad River.

Preacher Abel Gray smiled faintly at the old man. 'You refer to your drink as firewater, Mr. Smith. Isn't that the term generally used by Indians for hard liquor?'

'That it is!' Sam Smith agreed with a vigorous nod. 'But you don't need to worry any about Indians in South Wyoming.'

'Indeed?' Preacher Gray inquired politely.

'No, Reverend,' the old ex-miner said, 'we ain't had no trouble in this part of the state for a long spell; not since the Sioux finished off Custer in Montana.'

'That wasn't far away,' the preacher said.

'Nope. But we never did have trouble that bad here. And now the Indians are mighty quiet except for a flare-up now and then.'

'There sure has been more than one

3

flare-up lately around Mad River,' the man on the other side of the miner snapped. He was Flash Moran, a coarse type who'd grumbled and snarled ever since the stage had set out. The rest of the time he'd tried to get the attention of the preacher's daughter by leering at her. To her credit, she'd ignored him.

Sam Smith turned to the gambler, Moran, and said, 'I reckon those raids are going to peter out as soon as the sheriff finds out who is selling liquor to that Indian gang and puts a stop to it.'

The gambler in his pearl gray suit and matching bowler hat showed annoyance. Touching a corner of his generous black mustache, he said, 'Those drunken Sioux have put more than one small rancher out of business. And they're not finished yet.'

The Reverend Abel Gray looked concerned. 'Am I to understand that there have been Indian raids in the Mad River area?'

'An Indian gang,' old Sam Smith corrected him, and took another long haul from his bottle. 'An outlaw Indian gang is something different from tribes on the warpath. This is a bunch of redskins who have got a big thirst. And they pay for their booze by staging raids on some of the smaller ranches. They're a nuisance but not a state problem.'

The preacher frowned. 'Why doesn't your

4

local sheriff organize a posse and put an end to such lawlessness?'

Sam Smith chuckled. 'The way things have been in Mad River, Reverend, the sheriff has been plenty busy trying to keep law and order in the town. There's not been any spare time to police the countryside.'

The quiet, middle-aged preacher listened with interest. 'It sounds as if Mad River could use a church.'

Flash Moran gave a harsh laugh. 'You're dead wrong there, Reverend. You open another saloon and you'll do fine, but we ain't hankerin' to have any church. And we don't need any!'

The Reverend Abel Gray showed no resentment. 'I can tell that you are not interested in religion yourself, Mr. Moran. But there must be many in your frontier town who miss a church. A community should be balanced and cater to all.'

'Hear! Hear!' Old Sam Smith said cheerfully over his bottle as the wagon swayed wildly on a turn and sent him careening against Tim Parker again. 'I guess I got it in for you, young fella,' he said as the wagon came level once more.

With the attention turned to Tim, it was natural that the preacher should address himself to him. 'May I inquire what your business in Mad River is, Mr. Parker?'

Tim couldn't very well say he was a hired

gunman.

So he answered, 'I have no definite plans, sir. But I hope that some interesting work will show up.'

The girl, Sabrina, smiled at him and joined in the conversation for the first time, asking, 'Are you originally from Wyoming, Mr. Parker?'

'No,' Tim said. 'This is my first time in the state. I hail from Utah. But I've moved around a lot.'

Sam Smith chuckled. 'Reckon you must have, to wind up heading for Mad River. Why, it's the end of the world—not any place for a fine lad like you to look for a job.'

Flash Moran spoke up in his arrogant fashion. 'That's right. All you're liable to be offered in Mad River is work as a cowhand for one of the small outfits. And that can be poison both in money and saddle time, not to mention that the Sioux gang is always swooping down on the little owners. Must have been four or five went out of business in the last six months.'

Tim Parker gave the coarse man at the other end of the seat a cold glance. 'I figure I've been in a lot of worse spots.'

'Wait till you get there!' was the gambler's comment.

Preacher Abel Gray gave Tim a friendly glance and said, 'If you don't locate anything else, my daughter and I would be glad to have you pitch in and help us establish a church.'

Tim's smile was grim. 'I wouldn't make a good preacher.'

Sabrina smiled at him again. 'I'm sure my father wasn't seeing you in that role. But we always need someone to assist in a practical way. Money has to be raised and a building purchased or built. We can't do everything by ourselves.'

'I'll keep your offer in mind,' Tim promised.

Sam Smith had been draining the last of the whiskey from his bottle. Now he put it aside and addressed the preacher. 'Hope my drinking hasn't bothered you, Parson.'

Preacher Abel Gray smiled thinly. 'I believe temperance is the wisest course, but I do not try to impose my own beliefs on others.'

The grizzled old ex-prospector chuckled. 'Exactly my sentiments, Reverend. I say live and let live. But don't undervalue the importance of whiskey. I say it is the elixir of life.'

The blonde Sabrina's eyes twinkled. 'Isn't that rather a strong claim, Mr. Smith?'

'No, miss,' the old man with the black beard said solemnly. 'And I'll tell you how I come to believe what I do. When I was out on the trail alone, lookin' for the vein of gold that finally did come along, I used to get mighty lonesome.'

7

'I can well imagine that,' the girl agreed.

'So I started makin' friends of any of the Lord's livin' creatures that showed themselves around me,' Sam Smith went on seriously. 'Why, I once had a wolf trained just like a dog. And there was a gopher followed me around like a house cat. But the varmint I came to like the best was a frog I called Willie.'

Sabrina laughed. 'You make Willie sound like a very special frog.'

'He was,' Sam Smith assured her. 'Well, every night when I was sittin' alone by the campfire, this Willie would come out of the darkness and sit down near me. I'd be having a snort of whiskey to break the monotony, and after a few nights I noticed this Willie was watching me. He was lookin' at me mournful with his pop eyes and vibrating his throat like he hadn't had a drink in months. It was right pitiful.'

The Reverend Abel Gray raised his eyebrows. 'Are you suggesting the frog was begging you for alcohol? That would be poison to him.'

'Willie sure enough wanted a drink,' Sam Smith said. 'And I finally broke down and set some out for him in a saucer. Well, you never saw a frog lap anything up like he did that whiskey. And afterward he would sit there while I played the mouth organ and croak in a very musical fashion.'

8

Tim Parker exchanged a smile with the blonde girl.

She said, 'So you are musical, Mr. Smith? We must have you play for us at the church when we get it built.'

'If you can use a mouth organ soloist, I'm ready to oblige,' was the old man's reply. 'I only wish Willie the frog was here now to tell you how I played for him. It went on nearly every night for a month. We'd have our whiskey and then our musical evening together. He got so he could croak in almost every key to match my mouth organ. But like all good things, it had to come to an end.'

Preacher Abel Gray said, 'What broke you two up? Did you move on?'

'Nope, it wasn't that,' the old man said, 'though I was going to leave that section of the hills in a few days. What split us two friends wide apart was a lack of whiskey.'

'A lack of whiskey?' Sabrina questioned.

'That's what did it,' Sam Smith went on in his mock serious way. 'I didn't have enough for both of us, so I finished off the last bottle myself. Well, Willie just sat there, seemin' shocked and mournful. I couldn't look at those sad pop eyes. And when I began to play, he didn't croak at all. It got right to me, and I wondered what I could do to make him feel better. And it was then I remembered a bottle of sarsaparilla in my saddle bags. Now it wasn't alcoholic, but I figured Willie

9

wouldn't know the difference. So I went and dug it out for him and filled the saucer. And he brightened and lapped it up fast, just the same as always.'

Preacher Gray said, 'A step in the right direction for Willie. He was better off turning to temperance.'

Sam Smith gave the parson a bleak glance. 'Not exactly,' he said. 'When Willie finished off the sarsaparilla, I picked up my mouth organ and began to play, thinking he'd join in, croaking as usual. And then it happened.'

'What?' Sabrina asked.

'Willie gave the loudest burp you ever did hear and keeled over, as dead as a cucumber! And I ain't never touched sarsaparilla since,' Sam Smith said, jutting out his black beard.

Everyone in the lurching stage laughed except the gambler Flash Moran, whose red face showed disgust. There was silence for a little as each passenger returned to his own thoughts.

Tim's mind went back six years to the day when he'd been an easygoing small rancher in Utah. Newly married, he'd just finished a nice cabin for his attractive wife, Ella. He had ambitious plans to enlarge the ranch so that one day he'd have a stake to give the sons he hoped they would raise.

People liked him and he liked people. Ella and he had attended services in the tiny Baptist church in their town when the minister came on his monthly rounds. And there were square dances and house parties to make things lively and bring a break in the hard work.

Then everything changed for him. A deal to get some cattle at a low price took him out of town. While he was gone, his wife was attacked and killed and his cabin burned. A half-witted boy who'd been doing odd jobs and staying at the house with Ella ran off and hid. But he had seen who the killer was. And he stammered out the name to Tim when he came back home.

'It was One Eye! I seen him,' the boy said wildly, fear showing on his broad face at the memory of the violent moment.

Tim Parker had frozen, as cold as steel. 'You're sure?' he had asked the lad.

'I seen him! One Eye! He came toward me, and I knew he was going to kill me, too, so I ran!'

Tim was satisfied the lad had told him the truth. He told the tale to the sheriff and demanded that One Eye be arrested and tried for his wife's brutal murder. One Eye was a half-breed Sioux who worked for one of the wealthy ranchers. There was a rumor that he was the important man's half-brother.

The sheriff had heard Tim out in silence, and when he finished had frowned at him from behind his desk. 'I know how you feel, Tim. And everyone in town is sorry for you.

11

But I can't take action on the story of that half-witted lad. I can't arrest One Eye on his word.'

Tim couldn't believe it. 'Why not?' he demanded. 'The boy saw him. He's able to tell all that happened.'

'Boys like him make things up,' the sheriff said firmly. 'One Eye has an alibi for that night. Morton, the rancher who employs him, is willing to swear One Eye never left the ranch all night.'

Tim remembered the story about the half-breed and Morton being brothers. His anger mounting, he rose, saying, 'It seems that blood will tell. Morton isn't going to see One Eye swing. It could hurt his family pride.'

The sheriff flushed purple. He was an old, slow-moving and slow-talking man. He got to his feet and glared at Tim. 'I don't like to hear that kind of talk, Parker. You never caused any trouble around here before, and I hope you won't start any now.'

'I'm just asking for justice,' Tim declared. 'One Eye killed my wife. I want you to arrest him.'

'I can't do it,' the sheriff said stolidly. 'And I've told you why. The way I figure it, she was killed by some saddle tramp passing through here, and I'm investigating along those lines.'

Tim stared at him in angry disgust. 'You're

investigating along those lines when you know who the real killer is. And you won't charge him because Morton has warned you not to. And Morton is too big for you to buck in this county.'

'I do my duty as I see it,' the sheriff said grimly.

'Then arrest One Eye, or I'll go out to Morton's ranch and shoot him down myself!'

'You kill One Eye, and you'll swing for it.'

Tim shook his head. 'If someone had told me a story like this, I wouldn't have believed it. I thought this a decent town with decent people in it; that a person could live here in freedom and safety, knowing his family was protected; that there was a fair deal for everyone.' He laughed bitterly. 'And now I've got my fair deal!'

'You just take it easy, Tim,' the sheriff cautioned him. 'You let me look after administering the law here!'

'There is no law here!' Tim had snapped. And he'd walked out on the old man with his tarnished star. He'd headed straight out of town to the Morton spread, but when he got there One Eye had gone. And no one could say where.

That capped the climax for Tim. He wanted no more of the town, and he wanted no part of a rancher's life. Along with this change in his feelings had come a total lack of respect for the law. He knew he had to get

13

away. So he sold the ranch for half what it was worth to make a quick deal and then left Utah.

He'd roamed over most of the West since, but he'd never gone back to his native state. He'd tried to blot that happy past with Ella out of his mind. Only once in a while did he recall those days, usually when he was in the company of people who seemed decent and friendly.

It had been no accident that he'd decided to earn his living by his gun. The decision had been cold and deliberate. These days he lived in the present. There was no past and no future. He lived hard, and he didn't question whether his gun was used for wrong or right. He didn't believe in making that kind of moral judgment any more. In a ruthless world, he was living a ruthless life.

One other scar was carved deep in him as a result of Ella's murder. He hated Indians, especially half-breeds! He knew there was no logic in blaming all red men for the crime committed by one drunken half-breed, but that was the way it was.

His reverie was broken by Sam Smith, who thrust his black-bearded face toward Tim and said, 'You'll be interested in our sheriff in Mad River.'

Tim frowned. 'What makes you think so?' He began to wonder if the old prospector knew who he was and why he was going to

14

Mad River.

The old man chuckled wisely. 'I've just got a hunch, that's all.'

From his end of the seat, Flash Moran said, 'You'll find out a lot of things when you get to Mad River, Parker. It may make you change your mind about staying in the town.'

Tim Parker eyed him directly. He couldn't hide his dislike of the man in the pearl gray suit and bowler hat. 'I've never been scared off by a town yet.'

'You talk big,' Flash Moran said with a nasty smile that revealed a row of very even white teeth with a sparkling diamond set in one of the front ones. 'I'd say you won't last any longer than our preacher friend here. You'll probably both decide to take the next stage out.'

'If you manage, then I'm not worrying,' Tim said with open disgust. 'Most tinhorn gamblers I've met know enough to keep their mouths shut. Where did you learn different?'

Flash Moran's face went livid with anger. 'You and me will have a little discussion about that when the stage gets in.'

'Any time you like,' Tim Parker said evenly. 'But until then, just keep your nose out of my business.'

'You better be fast on the draw when we do our talking,' Flash Moran warned him. 'That's the kind of talk it will be.'

Tim Parker said nothing. Across from him,

he saw that Sabrina Gray was looking pale and alarmed. He was sorry he had been a party to an argument in front of the girl. But it was too late to do anything about that now.

Preacher Abel Gray addressed himself to Moran. 'You are wrong in thinking I'll give up easily in Mad River. I'm determined to establish a church in the town.'

Old Sam Smith leaned forward and glanced out of the stage window into the darkness. Then, chuckling, he told the preacher, 'Well, you'll soon have a chance to make up your minds. We'll be in Mad River in another five minutes!'

CHAPTER TWO

Tim Parker figured there would be nothing about Mad River that would be new to him. He'd seen too many small Western towns not to know the pattern. And as the stage rolled along the main street and the town gradually took shape, he was almost able to name the buildings before they came to them. There was more than one saloon, and even at this late hour lights blazed from their swinging doors. The hitching posts in front of these establishments were crowded with saddled horses and a few wagons.

Cowpokes still roamed the streets, some of

16

them staggering and boisterous, and Tim got the impression Mad River served as a gathering place for ranch hands from all over the area. They passed a bank, a general store and came to a halt before a dilapidated two-story frame building which bore an imposing black and white lettered sign above its verandah announcing it was the 'Mad River Hotel'.

The stage came to a jerking halt, and Sam Smith grinned at the others and said, 'Well, here we are. It's the end of the trail!'

Tim opened the door nearest him and stepped down into the street, where he waited to assist the pretty blonde Sabrina Gray, who rather timorously emerged next.

He held onto her black-gloved hand for a moment after she was safely on the ground and said, 'I enjoyed meeting you, Miss Gray. Hope I see you again.'

She managed a faint smile. 'Thank you.'

Preacher Abel Gray had now stepped down to join them. 'Thank you, Mr. Parker,' he said. 'Remember my offer. I'm going to need some help to bring the gospel to this town. And I do hope you don't get into any gun fight with that gambler.'

Tim's blue eyes held a twinkle. 'I reckon that's not likely,' he said. 'Far as I can tell, he's already left by the other door of the carriage.'

The preacher glanced around to check on

17

this and, finding it to be true, chuckled and turned to Tim again. 'There's no doubt you have the ability to measure a man. And that can be mighty important in my profession. Think over joining us.'

Tim Parker politely promised that he would and stood waiting for his bags to be unloaded as the preacher and his daughter went into the dingy hotel.

While he was standing there, the wizened old prospector came up to him and said, 'If you're thinking of staying at the hotel, I warn you its local name is Bedbug Manor.'

Tim smiled. 'Hope the reverend and his daughter don't have too bad an experience.'

The old man rubbed his short black beard speculatively. 'When Abe sees the cut of the preacher's collar, he's apt to be careful where he puts them. They got maybe one or two clean beds in the place in case the Governor or somebody special comes along.'

The stage drivers were still busily unloading the luggage and freight as they exchanged shouts and curses. Tim and the old man at last got their bags, and Tim asked, 'You have any suggestions where I can bunk tonight?'

'You can come out to the castle with me,' Sam Smith told him. 'I reckon there's a horse waiting for me at the livery stable. I told my Sioux boy to take care of it. And I can always rustle up another one.'

18

Tim hesitated. 'My business is in town. I've got to see someone first thing in the morning.'

'Mad River ain't but a half-hour ride from the castle,' the old prospector said. 'And I'd sure like to show you my place.'

Tim thought it over and decided he'd accept the old man's offer.

'Okay,' he said. 'If I can get a mount at the livery stable, I'll go along with you.'

'Don't you worry about it, son,' the old man said happily. 'Since it's this late, I don't see no need to go rushin' out to my place. Why don't we stop by the Lucky Palomino first and have a few drinks? I'm still mighty dry after that long ride.'

'Whatever you say,' Tim agreed. He wasn't tired, and he wanted to get the feel of the town.

They trudged down the main street with their bags in their hands. As they neared the entrance to the Lucky Palomino, Tim heard the familiar sounds of revelry, with a honky-tonk piano providing a background accompaniment. A few toughs and drunken loafers stood around on the sidewalk outside the saloon.

One of the bar bums came staggering up to Sam Smith and, with a wheedling smile, addressed the prospector in a reedy voice. 'Good to see you back, Sam! Can you lend me the price of a drink?'

19

The grizzled prospector halted and searched in his pocket for a coin which he gave the drunken man. He winked at him and reminded him, 'Don't bother me again tonight, Murphy.'

Murphy registered gratitude. 'Don't you worry about that, Sam!'

As they pushed their way through the swinging doors the prospector confided in Tim, 'One of the troubles about having a million dollars is that a lot of people think you ought to share it with them!' He led Tim over to an empty place at the bar, and they put their bags down and ordered.

The saloon crowd was beginning to thin out, but there were still a good many customers. The air was thick with tobacco smoke and the smell of liquor, and the remaining patrons were both drunk and noisy. Above the bar Tim noted a mural of a reclining nude and wondered if he'd ever hit a town where a saloon owner would be original enough to feature a painting of a horse above his bar. He hoped so.

But there was no denying the big saloon was well decorated. The bar was of shining mahogany, and the chandeliers were of cut glass and gave plenty of light. He took the shot of whiskey a surly bartender thrust at him and nodded to Sam Smith.

'Here's to your good health,' he said.

The bearded prospector nodded, downed

20

his own drink and then smacked his lips with satisfaction. 'It ain't easy to hang onto health in a town like this. You get mixed up with the wrong characters, and it's liable to leak out through a few bullet holes.'

Tin smiled. 'This place must be a money-maker.'

'A regular mint, though the sheriff has it on a black list and gives the owner considerable trouble.'

'Why?'

'There's a rumor going around town that the owners aren't too careful about who they supply with liquor.' The old man leaned close to Tim and in a low voice went on, 'The story goes that that gang of Indian outlaws get their liquor supply from this place through the back door.'

Tim raised his eyebrows. 'You think that's true?'

'I ain't got any idea,' Sam Smith said with a wise wink. 'I mind my own business, since I aim to stay healthy.'

'Who owns this place?'

'A syndicate headed by Jim Trent. They own a lot of the town, and they've gradually taken over most of the ranches. Story is the Union Pacific is coming through here, and land values are going to jump sky high.'

Tim was listening with wide open ears. He began to see why he'd been sent for. Evidently Mad River was going through a

21

chaotic period. And Jim Trent, who headed the syndicate owning this saloon and a lot of property, had hired him to help in the drive to take over the town completely. He had an idea Trent would want to pretend it was a legal operation, but behind the cover it would be the same old lawless swindle.

Not that he cared. The fact that renegade Indians were active in the area didn't please him too much. If they got in his way, he'd soon let them find out a white man could equal them in cunning and cruelty. He hoped that Jim Trent had brought him to the district to keep the Indians in line. That would be a job he'd really enjoy. But if Trent's saloon was selling liquor to them, it could be they didn't play any important part in Trent's schemes.

Helping himself to another drink from the bottle set out between him and Sam Smith, Tim asked, 'Is this Trent pretty well-liked around town?'

The old prospector shrugged. 'He's the mayor, if that means anything. A lot of folks owe him so much money they wouldn't dare vote for anyone else.'

'Then you wouldn't say he'd win in a popular vote?'

'Not a popular vote,' Sam Smith said sagely. 'But he got elected anyway, so that don't matter, does it?'

'I guess not,' Tim said with a slight frown.

'Now if the saloon is letting the Indians have liquor, that must make the sheriff pretty upset, especially since the mayor owns the saloon.'

'It does make for a touchy situation,' the old man with the beard agreed, 'when you consider that the sheriff was appointed by the mayor. But the mayor don't dare show that he'd like a change of law officer. He pretends to back Sheriff Slade and at the same time works against the office.'

'You've got the whole picture.'

'I watch and I listen,' Sam Smith said with a cunning smile. 'And I'm not as stupid as I look.' He poured them fresh drinks.

'I'd bet on that,' Tim said with a dour smile.

Sam Smith studied him with squinted eyes. 'Take you. I reckon I've got you figured right.'

'You think so?'

'Yep.'

'Go ahead,' Tim said. 'I'm listening.'

'You may have fooled that preacher and his gal, and even Flash Moran,' the old man with the beard said, 'but you didn't pull no wool over my eyes.'

'I'm just a lone cowpoke on a wandering trail.'

Sam Smith shook his head. 'I don't buy that, Mr. Parker.'

'Why not?'

'You ain't the type. And you're too sharp. I've seen plenty of drifters in my day. They've got an aimlessness about them. You can tell they ain't goin' nowhere special. But not you.'

'How am I different?'

'You got a look in your face and in your eyes. I'll bet you're a good hater. And I'd say maybe you came here to track somebody down and settle with them. And if I was the one you were after, I'd be mighty nervous.'

Tim smiled grimly. 'I can tell you that you've made a bad mistake. I'm not here for that.'

'Then somebody sent for you,' Sam Smith suggested slyly. 'Somebody has a job here for a smart six-gun toter like you to take care of.'

Tim knew he was on dangerous ground now. He said, 'I just came here because the stage was heading this way. We'd be better friends if you'd leave it at that.'

Sam Smith raised his glass. 'We'll play it your way,' he said as he downed the drink.

Tim turned around to study the far end of the saloon and at once saw a familiar face. Flash Moran was standing talking to one of the saloon girls and a big plug-ugly with a scar running across his forehead like the mark of a whip. It took only a minute for Tim to size up what was going on. Moran was agitating the big roughneck to cause some trouble.

24

He turned away from them and determined to start Sam Smith on his way as soon as possible. He wasn't hankering for any trouble the minute he hit town. Jim Trent wouldn't approve of that. When a gunman arrived to do a job, he attracted as little attention to himself as he could. This had become one of Tim's hard and fast rules.

He told Sam Smith, 'I'd like to get under way.'

'Just one more drink, son,' the thoroughly inebriated Smith said in a slurred voice, and poured out another round for them. Tim saw that he was going to have a problem getting out of the saloon and began to regret he'd gotten mixed up with the bearded man.

'This has to be the last one,' he warned the prospector as he raised his glass.

But he never finished the drink, for someone came up behind him and stumbled over his bag, then lurched against him so the whiskey splashed over his face instead of getting into his mouth. Tim swung around and saw the hulking thug whom Flash Moran had been setting up to cause trouble.

The big man snarled, 'You're mighty careless where you put your bag.'

'You aren't too smart about your walking,' was Tim's quiet reply. 'You could have avoided it just as everyone else has.'

'I don't aim to walk in circles to please you,' the big man said in a nasty tone.

'Let's just forget all about it,' Tim said, and turned his back on the big man to face the bar again.

'Look out, Parker!' Sam Smith suddenly cried out.

The warning came just seconds too late. The big man had grabbed Tim roughly by the shoulder and whirled him round. Then the big fellow planted a smashing right to Tim's face, catching him full on the lips and bringing blood as he staggered back against the bar.

The bully let out a great yell of delight and began to pummel Tim's body with both fists. The customers in the saloon gathered in a semicircle to watch the fight and shout encouragement to the bully. As Tim's head cleared, he realized he had to get away from the bar. The big man had him pinned there as a neat target.

He directed a weak left to the bully's jaw and, landing a glancing blow, took advantage of the split-second to edge quickly away from the bar. Now they were both in the open and sparring for advantage. Tim figured the bully was a hard puncher but with no true knowledge of the art of boxing. He crouched and moved in to land a solid right to the big fellow's heart, then followed it with a couple of quick lefts and rights to his body. It didn't seem to bother his opponent much. The bully came back and, aiming for Tim's head as

26

before, landed a stunning blow to his right ear.

Tim staggered again. But the blow had lost its full force before it got to him. Now he moved in and for the first time landed a strong punch on the big man's chin. It hurt! The bully's neck fairly cracked as he fell back. It was a good time for Tim to follow up, and he did. Another deft left caught the bully's eye and drew blood. In a few seconds the eye was puffed, and blood was making vision impossible.

Now the big man was really enraged, so much so that he came in swinging without any thought but to inflict damage on Tim. The crowd was fairly dancing with excitement, and Tim could hear Sam Smith's wheezy voice as he cried out encouragement to him. He felt the moment to settle with the bully was at hand. Neatly dodging most of the wild blows from the big fists, he darted in and landed an uppercut to the jaw that made the big man's eyes go glassy and his knees buckle.

Tim threw a fast left as the bully stared at him with dazed, unbelieving shock. Then, his face a pulpy mass, the big man crumpled in a heap on the floor. Tim stood over him grimly, but there was no more fight left in the stranger. In fact, he was completely out.

'All right, mister, that will do!' The words came in a feminine voice, and Tim glanced up to see that the crowd had given way to a young woman with stern but lovely features, dressed in a brown shirt and riding breeches, who held a gun in her hand—a gun pointed at Tim.

He stared at her in surprise. 'I only finished what he started,' he said.

The girl gave the man on the floor a grim glance and said, 'I know that.'

'Why are you mixing in this anyway?' Tim asked.

'I happen to be the sheriff in this town,' the girl said in a quiet tone of authority. She touched the silver star on her shirt with her free hand. 'I guess you didn't notice.'

Tim stared at the badge and gave a low whistle. 'I sure didn't.'

The gun was still pointed at him. 'You're a stranger in town, so I'll overlook this.'

'Mighty generous of you,' he said, 'especially since he started it.'

'No matter who starts a fight I hold both parties responsible,' the girl told him calmly. 'But I'll make an exception this time, providing you get out of here pronto!'

Sam Smith stepped up to her, carrying their bags. 'We're on our way this minute, Sheriff Slade.'

The girl frowned at the prospector. 'Is he a friend of yours?'

'You betcha!' Sam said proudly.

'I might have known it,' she told him with

28

a sigh. 'All your friends turn out to be trouble-makers.'

The little man with the black beard gave her an indignant look. 'That just ain't true, Sheriff.'

'Never mind,' the girl said wearily. 'Get him out of here before this one on the floor comes to.'

'Sure,' Sam Smith said. With a grin he turned to him and said, 'Come on, Tim. No more action here.'

Tim bent down and retrieved his Stetson from the floor. Smoothing his rumpled corn-silk hair, he put on the hat. He exchanged a grim glance with the attractive girl sheriff before following Sam Smith out. When they reached the wooden sidewalk and the cold night air, he gave the little man a wry look. 'You sure kept it a secret about the kind of sheriff Mad River has.'

'I gave you a hint, but you didn't take it.' Sam Smith chuckled. 'You shouldn't complain. She let you off scot-free.'

'But I didn't do anything but defend myself!' Tim protested.

'And you did that great,' the little man said happily. 'We'll go down the street to the livery stable and see what they've got in the way of horseflesh.'

As they walked along in the darkness side by side, Tim asked, 'How long has she been sheriff, and how did she get the job?'

'Quite a story,' the prospector said. 'Her paw had the job for years, and he was shot down taking a rustler prisoner. The town felt so bad they elected her in his place. They claimed they was doing it out of sympathy, but maybe they had other ideas.'

'Like what?'

'The deputy is an old man in his late sixties and don't amount to much. This gal does the best she can, but she can't handle the job like a man. I'd say some of the people who run things around here wanted Mad River to have a weak sheriff.'

'She handles a gun like she knows how to use it.'

'Make no mistake about that. She knows how.'

'Any of her folks live here?'

'Nope. She's alone. Her mother passed on of fever when she was just a little girl. So her Dad brought her up, more like a boy than a girl. Now she's on her own. And she has a lot of spunk. She's doin' well for a gal.'

Tim smiled bleakly. 'For a girl. But it's a crazy arrangement.'

'You'll get no argument from me,' Sam Smith declared. 'It's made Mad River a laughingstock. And it ain't helped law and order none.'

They had reached the livery stable. It had the familiar smell of horses, harness and smoke from the smithy's corner in about equal parts. Tim liked the odor and followed the old man to a room in the rear that served as an office. A lamp was burning feebly on a table in the small, cluttered room, and a middle-aged man in rough work clothes sat slumped in a chair, chin on his chest and snoring.

Sam Smith went over to the man and gave him a great whack on the back. 'Come to, you lazy blackguard,' he shouted. 'It's Sam Smith here for his horse.'

The sleepy man jumped up fast and blinked his eyes for a moment. Then he recognized Sam Smith. 'Sure, Mr. Smith, it's all saddled and ready for you. I'll go get him.' And he started out.

'Just a minute,' Sam Smith said. 'I'll need an extra mount for my friend.'

The stable man stared at him. 'I don't know, Mr. Smith. We're pretty short.'

Tim Parker thought he should speak for himself. 'I'm not particular. Anything with four legs will do. I'll be bringing it back early in the morning.'

'All right, mister,' the sleepy man said. 'I'll see what I can find for you.'

He did very well. The pinto he brought for Tim was perky enough to make him want to find out if he could make a deal for the piebald mare when he returned the next day. He and Sam Smith rode out of town together, heading for the old man's castle.

31

'They call it Smith's Folly,' the old man confided as they rode along. 'But that don't bother me any. A man's got a right to spend his hard-earned money the way he likes.'

'I'd say so,' Tim agreed.

'When I built the place, I thought I might marry me a wife one day,' the old man went on. 'But I guess it's too late for that. Any gal I like doesn't like me. I'm too old and they're too young. So I'm living there alone except for the passel of Injuns who look after me.'

Tim gave him a glance. 'Do you find them reliable help?'

'The best. Why would you think different?'

Tim shrugged. 'I don't much like Indians. Having them around me in a house would make me feel uneasy.'

Sam Smith turned to him in the saddle to eye him speculatively. 'Funny; you never struck me as a nervous man.'

'I don't think I'd call myself one.'

'What gives you this feeling about Indians?'

'I've got good reason,' Tim Parker said, staring ahead into the darkness, his mouth set in a grim line. They rode on in silence after that.

CHAPTER THREE

Tim didn't get much of a look at Smith's Folly that night. By the time he and the old prospector rolled in they were both completely exhausted. He was shown to a huge room on an upper level, and it was there he awoke early the next morning. The sun was streaming in, and he saw that the bedroom was furnished in elegant Italian Provincial style.

His reaction was wryly humorous. His rough Western attire and scanty bag of possessions were incongruous in the attractive big room. He realized that the entire castle was probably constructed and furnished on the same lavish scale. No wonder it had stunned the local people.

After he'd dressed, he went out on the balcony through French doors and studied the countryside. The castle's immediate surroundings were by no means attractive. It was rough brush country. But farther off there was a view of a blue and green mountain range that was surely impressive. He took a deep breath and wondered how old Sam Smith felt after his onerous journey and a night of hard drinking.

His answer came almost at once. From down below in the yard there issued a shout.

'How do you like it, Parker?'

He looked down and saw the little old man standing there smiling up at him. He laughed and said, 'I'll bet there's nothing like it anywhere else in this part of the country.'

'Guaranteed!' the prospector said with satisfaction. 'I had it copied from one of those Italian palaces. And the people who built it picked out all that furniture for me. It's the best, ain't it?'

'I've limited knowledge,' Tim said. 'But I'd be inclined to agree.'

'Come down and we'll have breakfast in the dining room,' Sam Smith said proudly.

The dining room proved to be huge, with a long table at which at least two dozen people could be seated. For breakfast Tim and the black-bearded little prospector sat at opposite ends of it. Tim had to stop himself from shouting at his host, Sam Smith appeared to be so far away. The breakfast itself was lavish, with plenty of ham and eggs. A silent middle-aged Indian waited on them. He entered and left the room soundlessly and gave Tim the creeps.

Sam Smith looked up from his plate of ham and eggs. 'Sure you can't stay here for a few days?'

'Sorry,' Tim said. 'I have to see some people.'

'You're welcome.'

'I know it. I think it's a fascinating place.

34

I've never seen anything like it.'

'Let me show you around at least before you leave,' the little man insisted.

And he did. Starting with the cavernous wine cellars, well-stocked with Europe's choice vintages, he led Tim through room after room. It was indeed a replica of a castle. Finally he showed his guest the turreted towers on the roof. The view from there was magnificent, even more impressive than the one Tim had enjoyed from his balcony.

'Spent a heap of money here,' was the old man's comment as he stared out toward the mountains. 'But a man has to have some project.'

'I think you spent your money well,' was Tim's opinion. 'I'd like to come back when I can spend more time.'

'You've got a standing invitation,' Sam Smith said seriously. 'And don't wait to hear from me. I don't go into town much any more. Come whenever you feel like it.'

'Thanks,' Tim said.

Sam Smith chuckled. 'And bring the preacher and his daughter along if you like. I saw you giving that gal the eye when we was in the stage.'

Jim asked, 'Do you think they'll last in town?'

'I wouldn't want to bet on it,' Sam Smith said. 'But you never can tell. He seemed pretty determined.'

'I noticed that. And the town should have a minister and a church.'

'We got a couple of traveling ones that come by every month or so and hold church in the courthouse, but I guess they won't count.'

'Not with the Reverend Gray.'

'Keep clear of Flash Moran,' Sam Smith warned. 'It's my guess he cooked up that trouble for you last night.'

'I'm sure of it. Does he work at the Lucky Palomino?'

'Maybe. Anyway, he's always around there.' The little man grinned. 'You'd best do what the preacher said and join up with him and that pretty young filly of his. You could do worse.'

Tim Parker's bronzed face with the pale blue eyes became somber. 'I had my share of domestic life. I don't aim to get myself mixed up permanent with a female ever again.'

The prospector winked. 'Lots of young men have made the same decision. But they fall into the trap sooner or later. Maybe you will, too.'

'Your sheriff interests me more,' Tim Parker said. 'What do you call her? Sheriff Slade or Miss Slade?'

'Her name is Susan,' Sam Smith told him. 'But she'll only let old coots like me call her by her first name. She'll be "Sheriff" to you.'

'Quite a girl,' Tim said, meaning it, 'even if

she probably is a rotten sheriff.'

The little man went out and saw him on the pinto mare, headed back to Mad River.

In daylight, Mad River looked even more ordinary than at night.

Tim rode the pinto straight to Trent's Hardware Store. He tied the mare to the hitching post and mounted the wooden sidewalk to enter the store. It was a long, rather narrow building, and not much light got inside. Its shelves were stocked high with every kind of merchandise, and a lot of things hung suspended over the counters from the ceiling. An apathetic young man, with straw wrist guards to protect his shirt and wearing thick glasses, came from behind a counter to serve him.

'What can I get you?' the young man asked.

'Nothing,' Tim said brusquely. 'I want to see Jim Trent.'

'You'd better come back,' was the clerk's comment.

Tim Parker frowned. 'I've come a long way to see him. I don't much like the idea of waiting.'

'He's busy.'

'He'll see me. Tell him Tim Parker is here.'

The clerk showed annoyance. 'I don't care who you are. He's in there having a meeting with Neilson and the judge, and he never wants anyone to bother him when they're here.'

'You take him word I'm here, or I'll do it myself,' was Tim's quiet warning.

The thin clerk looked a little nervous. 'It won't do any good,' he protested.

'You want me to go in there?' Tim took a step toward the rear of the store.

The clerk raised a restraining hand. 'I'll tell him. But he's going to raise Cain when I do.' And he hurried off unhappily to deliver Tim's message.

As he waited, Tim gave the situation some thought. This Neilson and the judge must be the others in the syndicate headed by Trent. These were the men who controlled the cow town.

The clerk came back with a bewildered expression on his pinched face. 'It's all right,' he said. 'You can go on back to Trent's office. It's up a couple of stairs to the rear.'

'I told you so,' Tim said with a grim smile. He had a dislike for stupid little men who enjoyed being officious.

Making his way along the shadowy aisle between the counters high with goods, he reached the steps and the glass-paned door that led into the private office of Jim Trent. He opened it, went inside and saw a dark, heavy-jowled man seated with his back to an open roll-top desk. In chairs near him were an enormously stout, bald man who must have weighed all of three hundred pounds and whose black suit did little to make him look slimmer, and a shriveled white-haired veteran in a frock coat, with a gaunt face, sharp, squinting eyes under bushy white brows, and a pendulous lower lip. All three of them were studying him with undisguised interest.

The dark, florid man at the desk, whose thinning black hair indicated he was the youngest of the trio, rose and stretched out a hand to Tim. He said, 'My name is Jim Trent. We've been expecting you.'

Tim shook hands. 'I got in late.'

'Not too late for a saloon brawl,' Jim Trent said, his cold eyes fixed on Tim. 'I heard about it.'

'That was too bad. But I didn't start it.'

'I know,' Jim Trent said, as if dismissing the subject. Turning to the other two men, who had remained seated, he added, 'These are my partners.' Indicating the enormously fat man, 'Neil Neilson, who is the town banker.' The shriveled sour one had his attention next. 'Judge Gordon Parsons of the local court.'

Tim nodded to the strange pair. 'Happy to meet you gents,' he said.

The stout banker had dainty white hands, surprising in a man of his great size. Folding them across his vest, he asked Tim, 'Have you ever worked in this part of the country

39

before?'

'Not within a hundred miles of here.'

The sour judge eyed him with bleak disillusionment. 'You made yourself less useful to us by getting into that brawl last night. I guess you know that.'

'I don't think any permanent damage has been done,' Tim said.

'And I'm inclined to agree, gentlemen,' Jim Trent said, taking a cigar from his vest pocket and biting the end from it. 'There may be certain benefits from the incident. It will give some of the boys around town the knowledge that Parker is not an easy mark.'

Banker Neil Neilson's moon face took on a happier expression. 'That is true, Jim,' he said in a squeaky voice. And to Tim, he added, 'If you plan to remain in Mad River, you'd do well to avoid Sam Smith. The old man is loco.'

Judge Gordon Parsons uttered a harsh laugh. 'That's the truth! Any man who'd put a fortune into a heap of rocks built on the edge of nowhere has to be crazy.'

Jim Trent lit his cigar and took a deep puff. 'We're not concerned with what Sam Smith does with his money, Parker. We just don't approve of you having anything to do with him while you're working for us.'

Tim gave the three partners a hard smile. 'Right at this moment I still haven't made a deal to work for anyone.'

40

There was an awkward silence. Then Jim Trent smiled. He said, 'You have us there, Parker. What's your price per month?'

Tim named a substantial sum. He'd doubled his last salary, thinking that he was on the edge of something big and knowing that the cunning three could well afford it.

Jim Trent removed the cigar from his mouth and stared at him. 'That's a lot of cash.'

Tim met his cold eyes. 'Experience never comes cheap.'

The fat banker spoke up from his chair. 'We can hire a half-dozen gunmen for that much money!'

Judge Parsons looked more shriveled than ever. 'And that's what we should do. You're too expensive for us, Parker.'

'I can always find work, gentlemen,' Tim said with a thin smile. 'No need to waste my time or yours arguing about price.' And he turned to leave.

'Parker!' It was Jim Trent who called to him to halt.

Jim turned. 'Yes?'

'We'll meet your price,' Jim Trent said. 'It's a holdup, but we need a man like you.'

'In that case, it can hardly be termed a holdup,' Tim Parker said with a disdainful smile.

The fat banker looked up at him with greedy eyes. 'We'll expect complete loyalty

41

from you, Parker. And we'll want you to do as we say without asking questions.'

'I understand,' Tim said. Judge Gordon Parsons leaned forward in his chair and pointed a shaky finger at him. 'No matter what happens,' the judge said, 'you don't know me. I have nothing to do with your employment, and I can't offer you favors from the bench. The law is above compromise.'

Tim studied him with a bitter expression. 'I'm familiar with the law.'

Jim Trent spoke up in somewhat apologetic fashion. 'The judge doesn't mean he won't do anything he can to make your work easier. He will. He will do his best to protect you at every turn. But if any embarrassing accident should occur, you aren't to mention your relationship to him.'

'Short of having my neck stretched, I'm not liable to forget,' Tim told them.

'You'll not be in any danger like that,' Jim Trent said urbanely. 'Your job is going to be managing the Lucky Palomino for us. The last man we had was not trustworthy and met his death rather suddenly. We need someone we can depend on completely to head the operation. It is more complicated than it seems on the surface.'

Tim asked, 'Will Flash Moran be working under me?'

Jim Trent nodded. 'Flash is our table man.

42

He knows how to run a paying poker game, though otherwise he's stupid. He'll go on working as usual, but he'll be warned to get along with you. And he'll do it.'

'Just so he remembers that,' Tim said firmly.

'If he doesn't, we'll get rid of him,' Jim Trent promised. 'He's not important to our set-up.'

'What is your set-up?' Tim wanted to know.

'I'm not ready to tell you more right now,' Trent said. 'We've given you your price, and we've told you where and how you start work. That's all you need to know at present.'

'I see,' Tim said.

The fat banker, Neil Neilson, spoke up. 'Just look after your job and don't try to cheat on us, and you'll have no trouble.'

'And keep out of arguments with Sheriff Slade,' Judge Parsons said in his angry, quvering voice. 'We don't want any more interference from her.'

'That is a sore point,' Jim Trent agreed, turning to Tim. 'As you found out last night, we have a young woman acting as sheriff. She takes the job pretty seriously and her deputy does whatever she tells him to. She's not exactly in love with our Lucky Palomino operation, and so anything you can do to make her happy will be a help.'

43

'I'll keep that in mind,' Tim promised.

'We've thought of finding another sheriff one day,' Jim Trent went on smoothly. 'And it could be you'd be a good choice if you make out well in this job.'

'Thanks,' Tim said quietly. 'Anything else?'

'Not now,' Jim Trent said, those cold eyes studying him. 'You are as fast with a .44 as they claim, aren't you?'

'I manage.'

'That's a comforting thought,' Jim Trent said. 'In time you'll have your chance to show us your skill. You may as well go over to the Lucky Palomino now and let them know you're taking charge.'

'Are they expecting me?'

Trent nodded. 'Everything's arranged. Good luck, Parker.'

'Yes,' Tim said. He bowed to the fat man and the dried-up judge. 'Interesting meeting you two gentlemen.'

He left the office and walked out through the store. The young clerk peered at him from the shadows behind the counter with a baleful expression on his white face. Tim moved to the door and out into the sunshine.

He stood in the warm sun for a minute, grateful for the fresh air after being in the office.

'Mr. Parker!' It was the Reverend Abel Gray, who had seen him from across the

44

street and was now hurrying over to join him. 'I'm glad to see you again,' the gray-haired clergyman said as he came up beside him.

'You're still here,' Tim said with a smile.

'Indeed I am. My daughter and I intend to stay, though not in that filthy hotel.'

'I hear it has a bad reputation.'

'Disgraceful place,' the preacher said with disgust. 'Sabrina and I left there early this morning.'

'Sorry I didn't get a chance to warn you about it,' Tim said. 'I didn't hear the full story until after you'd gone in.'

'Quite understandable,' the clergyman said. 'You are a stranger here, like ourselves. May I say that Sabrina enjoyed meeting you a great deal? She doesn't have much opportunity to meet young men in a social way. The stage journey provided a splendid chance for this.'

Tim felt ill at ease. He hoped the clergyman wasn't trying to be a matchmaker. But he had to be polite and say, 'I'd judge her to be a fine girl.'

'Wonderful! Wait until you get to know her better. And she's so practical. Already she has found us a home and a temporary church.'

Tim smiled in spite of himself. 'That's fast work,' he said.

'It's somewhat simpler than it sounds,' the Reverend Abel Gray admitted. 'She learned about an empty store down the street. There

45

are modest living quarters in the rear of it. So we shall make our home in the back and conduct our mission in the store itself until we are ready to move to larger quarters.'

'That's great,' Tim said. 'I'd say a church could do a lot of good here.'

'I've already learned that. You have no idea of the lawlessness that is rampant in this small city, and not only among the white men. The Indians are being badly abused.'

'Oh?' It was a subject Tim wanted to avoid.

'I have great sympathy for the Indian people,' the clergyman went on, seemingly unaware of Tim's coolness.

'From what I hear, they've been causing trouble here,' Tim said. 'I understand a renegade band has been raiding the small ranchers.'

'I suspect Indians may not be to blame,' the Reverend Abel Gray told him. 'At least from the little information I've gathered in this short time, that is my impression. Someone could be urging them to take this kind of action. They are a simple folk and can be misled easily.'

'I wonder,' Tim said dryly. 'If you'll excuse me, I've got to take this mare back to the livery stable. I only had her for the night.'

'Of course.' The clergyman beamed. 'Forgive me for taking your time. But I did want to tell you the good news.'

'I'm glad to hear it.'

46

'And do come and see my daughter and myself if you stay in Mad River,' the clergyman insisted. 'Have you decided about remaining?'

Tim hesitated. 'Yes, I'm staying, Reverend. I'm taking over as manager of the Palomino Saloon.'

Reverend Abel Gray looked surprised. 'The Lucky Palomino?'

'That's it.'

'I'm a little astonished,' the older man said. 'Somehow I didn't see you as the person for that sort of work.'

'Sorry to disappoint you, Reverend,' Tim said, and stepped down from the sidewalk to mount the pinto.

The clergyman remained standing on the wooden sidewalk, looking rather forlorn. He called out, 'I hope this doesn't mean the end of our friendship.'

'It shouldn't have to,' Tim said from the saddle.

'So do come and see the mission. Sabrina will be looking forward to your visit.'

'Thanks,' Tim said. He nudged the mare on down the street.

CHAPTER FOUR

It didn't take Tim too long to work out a deal at the livery stable. He paid for the pinto mare and then rode back to the Lucky Palomino. The three-story building looked gray and drab in daylight, and the sidewalk in front of its swinging doors was deserted. Tim tied the mare to the hitching post and went inside. The saloon was shadowy and empty except for a surly bald bartender who stood leaning on the bar, glaring at him.

Tim went over to the bar and said, 'Business is slow.'

'There ain't none at this time of day,' the bartender told him in a harsh voice.

'I suppose not. Let me introduce myself. I'm Tim Parker, your new boss.'

The surly man continued to glare at him. 'Another one? Trent ain't had much luck keeping his managers healthy lately.'

Tim's smile was tight. 'I've got perfect health.'

'Mind you don't lose it.'

'Is Flash Moran around?'

The bald man indicated the rear with a nod. 'In the office.' He gave Tim a nasty grin. 'I suppose it's your office now.'

'I suppose so. Thanks.'

He came to a door marked, 'Private,

Manager', and swung it open. He saw Flash
Moran seated behind a cluttered desk, talking
to a younger man who was plainly a
half-breed. The half-breed glanced up at Tim
nervously. He had a shifty face and seemed
upset at being found with the gambler. He
jumped up quickly.

At the same time Flash Moran rose with a
scowl. 'Don't you ever knock before you bust
into a private office?'

'Not when it's my office.'

Moran showed astonishment. 'You're Tim
Parker?'

'Right.' Tim nodded at the half-breed.
'Who is this and what's he doing here?

'His business is with me personal,' Moran
snapped. And to the half-breed, 'Okay, Slim,
you can go now.'

The half-breed gave the gambler a
meaningful glance, then turned and hurried
out by Tim. Tim wasn't too happy about the
half-breed being there but decided he
wouldn't make an issue of it right away.

He said, 'I guess Trent sent you word I was
taking over.'

'Yeah, he did,' Flash Moran said, studying
him through narrowed eyes. 'He told me the
new boss was going to be Tim Parker, but he
didn't bother to let me know it was you.'

'Maybe he thought it would be better for
you to find out for yourself,' Tim suggested.

'Maybe.'

'Since we're to be working together, I think we should clear the slate,' Tim said. 'What happened last night should be allowed to rest.'

The coarse face of the gambler showed a nasty grin. 'Suits me.'

Tim's jaw was set in a stern line. 'I'm not expecting any more of the same from you or your friends.'

'I don't know what you're talking about.' Moran's tone was mocking.

'I reckon you do,' Tim insisted. 'But we'll let it go at that. You do your job, and you'll have no trouble from me.'

Moran said, 'I'm handling the tables for Jim Trent, and that's who I'll report to.'

'Whatever Trent says,' was Tim's reply. 'Meanwhile, this is my office, and I will be running the Lucky Palomino.'

Flash Moran moved around from behind the desk. 'You better be lucky. This place has had a big turnover in managers.'

'I aim to make it a permanent job until I decide to move on.'

The gambler chuckled harshly. 'Maybe you'll move on quicker than you expect.'

'Don't count on it,' Tim told him. 'And while I am in charge, I'm making some new rules. The saloon is off bounds to Indians, and that includes half-breeds like your friend Slim.'

Moran lost his good humor fast. 'Maybe

Trent will have something to say about that.'

'If he does, he can say it to me,' Tim said. 'Now you'll oblige me by getting out of here pronto. Since it is suppposed to be my private office, I'd like to enjoy a mite of privacy.'

Moran gave him an ugly look. Then with a shrug he turned, went out and slammed the door shut after him.

Tim stared at the door for a second, then moved around behind the desk and sat down.

For the next half-hour he kept busy going through the desk and making what sense he could of the books he found there. Whatever the merits of his predecessors might have been, they hadn't shown any talents along bookkeeping lines. The records of the Lucky Palomino were in a mess. He figured it was a job where being handy with a gun was all that counted. Trent probably took care of all the necessary accounts.

He'd barely come to this conclusion when there was a knock on his door and he invited whoever it was to come in. The door opened, and a stranger presented himself. The newcomer was squat and grizzled, with a broad purple face and bushy gray eyebrows shading tired eyes. He looked like a man who was weary of the trail, and he wore a deputy's badge.

Standing before Tim's desk, he announced himself in a rasping voice. 'Deputy Pete Holm. The sheriff sent me over.'

51

'Oh?'

'Yep. She wants to see you.'

'Then why didn't she come here herself?'

The deputy looked bleak. 'When the law gives you an invitation, it's usually wise to accept it.'

'Any idea why she wants to see me?'

'She knows you're the new manager of the Lucky Palomino, and she wants to get a few things straight.'

Tim smiled grimly. 'News gets around Mad River fast.'

'It's a small town.'

'So it seems,' Tim said with a hint of irony. 'I'm so new to all this that I don't think there's much point in my talking to the sheriff yet.'

'Maybe her judgement on that is better than yours,' the veteran deputy hinted.

Tim stared up at the old man's lined face. 'Is she at the jailhouse now?'

'Yep. She's waiting in her office.'

Tim nodded. 'You can tell her I'll be over presently.'

'Take my advice, mister, and come as soon as you can,' the deputy said. 'The sooner you hear what she has to say, the better it might be for you.'

'Thanks,' Tim said.

The deputy didn't linger. He went out, leaving the door open behind him.

Tim didn't much like being regally

summoned to the sheriff's office, but he decided to follow the deputy's advice and find out what the girl wearing a sheriff's star had to say.

Out in the blazing sun of the street, he was about to mount the pinto when he heard a crash of glass. He paused to turn and saw that someone had fallen through the window of the store where the Reverend Abel Gray and his daughter had set up their church. Whoever it was now lay sprawled on the wooden sidewalk. Tim left the pinto and went over to see what had happened.

A small crowd was already gathering before the storefront. By the time Tim reached the board sidewalk outside the broken window, the Reverend Abel Gray and Sabrina had also appeared.

Seeing Tim, the blonde Sabrina ran to meet him. 'A dreadful thing just happened, Mr. Parker. A drunken Indian came into the mission, and when my father tried to reason with him he put up resistance. In the struggle that followed, he toppled out of the window.'

'He couldn't have been very steady on his feet to start with,' was Tim's comment.

'He was terribly drunk,' Sabrina assured him.

Tim pushed his way through the crowd in time to see the half-breed, Slim, helping the fallen man to his feet. Slim saw him, and a frightened look crossed the half-breed's face.

He dragged the still hopelessly drunk Indian off quickly as the crowd guffawed.

Looking badly upset, the Reverend Abel Gray turned to Tim. 'We haven't gotten off to a very good start,' he said.

'You shouldn't have tangled with that drunken Injun,' Tim said in disgust. 'They can be mean.'

'This one was almost paralyzed by liquor,' the preacher said. 'There was no struggle. I tried to turn him around to get him out when he all at once fell against the window.'

'When we replace the glass, I'll cover it with chicken wire,' Sabrina said.

Tim gave her a rueful smile. 'You're still going ahead, knowing what this town is like?'

The Reverend Abel Gray said, 'We expect some unpleasantness, Mr. Parker.'

'You're liable to get a good deal more than some,' was Tim's warning. 'This town is ripe for an explosion.'

The preacher gazed at him with a concerned expression. 'At least I can agree with you on that,' he said. 'I've seen enough of these towns to be aware that something is breeding here. You should have an idea what it is. What's your opinion?'

Tim was wary. 'I'm not paid to have opinions.'

Sabrina's pretty face showed disappointment. 'We forgot about your new job,' she said. 'I suppose you are working for them, whoever they are.'

'Them?' Tim questioned.

The Reverend Abel Gray spoke up. 'My daughter is referring to the persons responsible for the evil in Mad River. We've been told the Lucky Palomino is where most of the Indians get their liquor. And you are the new manager.'

'I'll be making some changes at the Lucky Palomino,' Tim said in a taut voice.

Sabrina Gray's face brightened. 'I'm glad to hear that, Mr. Parker,' she said. 'I've felt from the beginning we could count on you to do the right thing.'

Tim smiled sourly. 'I'm not ripe for conversion, if that's what you have in mind, miss. But I've a strong dislike for Indians generally, and I know they're plumb crazy when they get liquor. For that reason I'm making sure the Lucky Palomino bars them as customers.'

'That could be a beginning,' the Reverend Abel Gray said. 'Most of the trouble in the area is being caused by Indians.'

'I still think you'd be wise to get on the next stage out of here,' was Tim's advice. 'Mad River isn't ready for a church yet.' With a brusque nod he turned and left them standing in front of the shattered window.

Tim swung up onto the mare and rode down the dusty street toward the jailhouse.

It was a single-story stone building. Tim

55

mounted the worn steps and went inside. The office was small, with a single roll-top desk. Sheriff Susan Slade was sitting at it writing when he entered.

She turned around to look at him with an interested expression, and he had his first good chance to study her. She was dark-haired, with large brown eyes and olive skin.

She greeted him quietly. 'Thanks for coming.'

He smiled thinly. 'Your deputy didn't leave me much choice.'

Still seated in the swivel chair, she continued to appraise him with those serious brown eyes. 'Pete can be pretty direct. He may have made it sound like an order. It was only a request.'

He stood there, conscious of her eyes on him. 'I'm here.'

'Yes,' she said, as if that settled it. Then, rolling the pen she was holding between the fingers of her right hand, she told him, 'When I found you brawling in the Lucky Palomino last night, you didn't tell me you were the new manager.'

'I didn't know it then.'

Her eyebrows rose. 'Trent couldn't have made up his mind about you that quickly,' she said. 'You must have come to Mad River on his orders.'

'He sent for me,' Tim admitted. 'But I

56

didn't know what my job was to be. Otherwise I wouldn't have gone into the saloon with Sam Smith.'

Susan Slade showed grim amusement. 'Sam Smith is pretty much of a character.'

'So I've been told.'

'That crazy old man nearly always spells trouble when he's in town,' the girl sheriff said. 'Still, I like him.'

'So do I.'

She got up and stood facing him. She was a good head shorter than he. She said, 'I can't say the same thing about your new boss. Jim Trent is behind most of the trouble in Mad River.'

'I wouldn't know about that.'

'I'm telling you.'

'I still wouldn't know,' he said stolidly.

Her smile was bitter. 'When you came in here just now, it seemed to me you might be more than just another renegade with a gun for hire. I guess I was wrong.'

Tim shrugged. 'I was brought here to do a job, and I'm going to do it. It's as simple as that.'

'Have you any idea what kind of job it is?'

'I reckon so.'

Her eyes were sharp now. 'You'll be doing more than running the Lucky Palomino. You'll be responsible for a lot of Jim Trent's underhanded activities.'

He showed no expression. 'Trent hasn't

57

told me any more than that I'm to keep things running smoothly at the Lucky Palomino. How can you know so much about what he expects?'

'Because I've been in Mad River longer than you have,' she said, 'and because old Pete and I are the only law this town has. I'm pretty familiar with the rotten soft spots here, Mr. Parker. And I can tell you right off the Lucky Palomino is one of them.'

'Go on,' he said. 'You interest me.'

The girl sheriff took a deep breath and eyed him defiantly. 'I asked you here, hoping to warn you off. Mad River doesn't need any more of Trent's hired gunmen. Why don't you pass up this job and travel on?'

He laughed curtly. 'I'm staying. Trent is paying me well.'

'Why not?' she asked with contempt. 'He can afford to. He's playing for big stakes. I see I was wrong in my hunch about you. You're like Flash Moran and the rest of Trent's outlaw bunch.'

'Aren't you talking pretty wild?' he asked. 'All I know is that Trent is a respected businessman and the mayor. And he seems to have some pretty important friends.'

Susan Slade's lip curled. 'If you're thinking of the banker and the judge, they are bigger crooks than Trent. He covers for them. And they're all banded together to drive out the small ranchers and blame it on the Indians.

58

That's why the Lucky Palomino makes it their business to see the redskins get all the liquor they want!'

Tim at least knew where he stood on this. Meeting her derisive eyes with a firm glance, he said, 'While I'm managing the Lucky Palomino, there won't be any liquor sold to Indians.

The girl sheriff looked astonished, and then her expression changed to one of distrust. 'That's easy to say.'

'I mean it.'

'You'll have a chance to prove it.'

'I will.'

Her attractive face now showed new interest. 'You do talk as if you weren't fooling about it.'

'I'm not.'

'Have you spoken to Trent about it?'

'Not yet.'

She shook her head. 'Then you've a surprise coming. You'll be selling liquor to the redskins and liking it.'

'If that's the deal, then I will be moving on.'

She stood there with a hand on her hip and an admiring expression on her attractive face. 'So you do have some principles after all?'

'I'm firm on that. I happen not to trust Indians. I've had my fill of the noble red man!'

Susan Slade stared at him. 'You feel pretty

strongly against Indians, don't you!'

'I despise them.'

'I guessed that,' she said. 'I think it's pretty silly, but I suppose you have your reasons.'

'I have,' he said grimly. 'And they're not silly.'

'I wouldn't expect you to think so,' the girl sheriff said. 'I had you all wrong for a while there. I figured you were against selling booze to the Indians on principle, because its forbidden by law and not fair to them. But I see now that isn't the case at all. With you it's something personal. You hate your red brothers and won't tolerate them around you even in a dump like the Lucky Palomino.'

His cheeks were burning. 'You can put it that way if you like.'

'It's the only way,' she said. 'I'm all for your keeping the Indians out of the saloon, but I can't go along with your reasons for doing it.'

'Don't worry about it!'

'But I do,' she insisted with a frown, 'because Indians are being wrongly blamed for a lot of the raids going on against the small ranchers. Trent and his outfit are using some renegade half-breeds as a front for their own outlaw gangs.'

'Any proof of that?'

'I aim to have some soon,' she said. 'Trent is using Wolf and a few others to keep some of the Indians crazy drunk so they seem guilty of the attacks on the small ranching outfits. And it's not the Indians at all.'

'I'm not interested,' he said. 'But I won't have them in the saloon while I'm running it.'

'I think you will,' she said, 'if you're going to be Trent's man.'

'I'm nobody's man but my own,' he said angrily. And he turned and walked out of the office.

CHAPTER FIVE

Whatever Tim might think of Susan Slade as sheriff, he couldn't help admiring her as a young woman. She had spunk, and she hadn't been afraid to tell him exactly what she thought. He realized the only way he could get off to a proper start in Mad River was to have a clear understanding with Jim Trent. So he rode straight back to the general hardware store to see him again.

This time Trent was alone in his office when Tim stepped inside to talk to him. The powerfully built man with the thinning dark hair glanced up at him with a slight frown.

'Something wrong already?'

'Maybe.'

Trent continued to stare at him. 'I don't like to be bothered with saloon business during store hours,' he said. 'I generally come over for a nightly check on things. Otherwise I expect you to operate on your own.'

Tim took this in his stride. 'I understand that,' he said. 'But right now I'm not sure I want to manage the Lucky Palomino.'

Trent removed the cigar he was smoking from his mouth and looked astonished. 'But you've already taken the job at a salary twice what we intended to pay!'

Tim smiled thinly. 'I didn't know then that part of my job was to let any Indians who wanted to liquor up there.'

Trent's eyes narrowed. 'Who have you been talking to?'

'A lot of people. It seems to be pretty well known in town that any of these renegade Sioux can get all the liquor they want through the back door of the Lucky Palomino.'

'That bothers you?'

'Indians bother me! I don't want to have anything to do with them. If that's part of the job, I don't want it.'

Trent considered for a moment. Very deliberately he placed the fat cigar between his heavy lips again and took a deep puff on it. Then he gave Tim a shifty glance. 'You didn't say anything about that when we took you on.'

'I wasn't sure then what was going on at the Lucky Palomino.'

'You can't be sure of it now,' Trent countered.

'I'm sure enough.'

'Okay,' Trent said. 'You needn't worry about the Indians. I'll pass the word we won't be looking after them in future. That satisfy you?'

'We'll see. Another thing. Flash Moran doesn't cotton to me. Says he intends to report to you and no one else.'

Trent tapped the ash from his cigar. 'Let it go at that. He's a smart man at the tables. I'd prefer to keep him. I'll talk to him about it. No reason he shouldn't work directly with me.'

Tim's look was bleak. 'It means I won't have any control over him. He could give me trouble. And I'll take no responsibility for anything he does.'

'That will be all right,' Trent said too easily. 'Anything else bothering you?'

'Not right this minute.'

'Then everything's settled,' the black-haired man said with a smug look on his coarse face. 'Seems to me you've got a lot of scruples for a gunman. I'd try to get rid of a few of them. Better for your business.'

'I've done all right so far,' Tim Parker told the mayor of Mad River. And he left him without saying anything more.

Business was good at the saloon on this first night Tim was in charge. The bar was lined with thirsty cowpokes, and the tables were filled as well. In the rear, Flash Moran

63

presided over the house poker game and had a full complement of players. Baldy, the piano player, tinkled the ivories, and loud talk and laughter gave the long, smoked-filled room a jovial atmosphere.

Tim had taken a stand near the main entrance of the saloon and greeted the patrons as they came in. The regulars soon introduced themselves to him, and he was accepted as the new boss. Now and then he was aware of a furtive second look from some of the patrons, as if they wanted to size him up before anything happened. Being well aware of the mortality rate of former managers of the place, he wasn't bothered by their unconcealed curiosity.

The bartenders knew their jobs and kept busy. Herb, the head bartender, seemed to have taken a dislike to Tim and avoided him as much as possible. When the game at the poker table ended, Tim saw the bartender make his way across the crowded room and hold a furtive conversation with Flash Moran. While the two talked, Moran kept an eye on Tim.

Herb left the gambler and vanished out back somewhere. Tim was ready to follow him to see if he could find where he'd gone when a group of rowdy patrons came pushing in through the swinging doors. One of them was the big tough he'd manhandled the night before. They pushed past him and made for the bar. The big man pretended not to have seen him, but Tim knew this was merely pretense on his part. However, he decided to let it go as long as the outlaw made no trouble.

The tough's face still showed marks of their battle as he leaned on the bar and loudly ordered a drink. Tim knew he couldn't leave the floor now that this crowd of troublemakers had arrived. He'd have to postpone finding out what Herb and Flash Moran were up to. He maintained his stand by the door, with his hand on his .44. Every now and then one of the group with the big tough would glance his way and make some comment too low-pitched for him to hear, and then there would be laughter.

He was still by the swinging doors when veteran Deputy Pete Holm came striding in. The old man gave him a wise look. 'Everything under control here?'

'Just as you see it,' Tim told him.

The grizzled deputy eyed the crowd. 'You got a full house.'

'Sure,' Tim said. 'And everyone is having a good time.'

The weary, lined face of the deputy relaxed. 'The calm before a storm.'

'I don't think so,' Tim said, though he was by no means as sure as he tried to sound.

Deputy Pete Holm said 'I heard some loose talk in the street that Red Barnes is fixin' to get even with you for bashin' him up last night.'

Tim glanced over and saw that the big tough was glancing over his shoulder at them. His eyes on the bruised face of Red Barnes, he told the deputy, 'I would think he'd gotten himself enough punishment without asking for more.'

'Tonight he's got friends to help him,' the deputy warned.

'You're saying I might have to take on the whole gang?'

'That bunch stays close together,' the deputy said. 'I've known them to settle a grudge with teamwork before.'

'Thanks for the tip.'

'Part of my job as law officer,' the deputy said. 'We don't play no favorites. The idea is to keep the peace in town. Savvy?'

'I savvy,' Tim said grimly, his eyes still on the outlaw, Red, who had begun conferring with his friends at the bar. 'I just hope he does.'

The grizzled deputy said, 'I wouldn't count on that. And I'd be careful to stay in here. They're not liable to gang up on you unless you start scrapping with them in the street.'

'I'll remember that.'

'Not that you deserve any good advice,' the deputy growled. 'You've come in here as Trent's trained gunslinger. That means you're no asset to the town.'

66

Tim gave him a sour grin. 'I'm surprised to hear you talk about your mayor like that.'

'He wasn't my choice for mayor,' Pete Holm declared. 'None of the law-abiding folk wanted him, but there were enough votes on the other side to elect him.'

'Proving that Mad River is essentially a lawless town.'

'Proving that Trent knew how to stuff the ballot boxes with crooked votes,' the deputy growled. 'He's brought you in to make trouble for Sheriff Slade, and there's no mistake about that.'

Tim showed surprise. 'I don't know why you say that. I like Miss Slade.'

Pete Holm purpled. 'No need to remind me the sheriff is a miss! But that don't make her any less fit for office. Her paw was the best marshal in these parts. Until he was shot in the back by a no-account rustler, he kept law and order in Mad River. And I aim to give his daughter the same support I gave him. Don't get the idea that gal don't know her job.'

'I didn't say that.'

'But you meant it just the same,' the old man said angrily. 'It could be that before you finish here, you'll be glad to have the sheriff's help.'

'It could well be,' Tim agreed, glancing across at Red Barnes again.

'I reckon the sheriff warned you about

67

feedin' them Sioux liquor,' the deputy went on. 'And I'll just add that if we catch you at it, you'll get the full penalty of the law.'

'You needn't worry.'

'We'll see about that,' Pete Holm said in a warning tone, and left by the swinging doors.

The talk and laughter became more subdued. Flash Moran, standing at the end of the bar, was studying Tim with a mocking smile on his bloated face. Baldy's ragtime on the out-of-tune piano sounded louder. Faces turned toward Tim expectantly. He knew something had to break soon.

It happened quickly. Red Barnes swung around from the bar with his filled whiskey glass in a beefy hand. The battered, ugly face showed a nasty smile. Then he came lumbering across the big room to stand before Tim.

'Hear you're the new boss of this place,' he challenged him.

'What about it?' Tim asked evenly.

Red Barnes sneered. 'I'll tell you what about it! Your whiskey is rotten! Nothin' but rotgut!' And he underlined this by hurling the contents of the glass at Tim's face.

In a taut voice Tim said, 'I licked you good last night. So I'll let this go as part payment on that. If you don't like the liquor, get out!'

The big tough leered at him. 'You beat me last night because I was too drunk to fight back. I'd like to tangle with you right now,

68

but you're too yellow!' And he gave Tim a shove.

The crowd let out a yell of encouragement, and Tim was suddenly aware he was being placed in a bad spot.

Quietly he said, 'All right, Barnes. If you're itching for another beating, I'll oblige.'

'Soon as you get rid of your .44 and I unsling my shootin' irons, we can mix it up outside,' the big man said.

Tim remembered the deputy's warning not to try to battle Barnes outside lest he find himself fighting the whole gang. But that didn't help now. He had no choice but to accept the challenge.

'Suits me,' Tim said. He unhooked the belt holding the .44 and passed it to one of the saloon girls who had come up to watch the show.

Red Barnes tossed his gun belt and weapons to one of his cronies. The crowd surged toward the door as Barnes led the way out.

Tim followed him, swept along with the crowd. In the semi-darkness of the street, the crowd formed a circle around the two men and shouted for them to begin the battle. Tim circled a little as the big outlaw crouched and came warily toward him. In the background a horse whinnied, and there was the restless pounding of hooves as the animals at the nearby hitching post smelled danger in the cool night air.

Red Barnes made the first real move. He came at Tim with arms flailing and landed some clumsy blows to his body. Tim dodged back to miss the full force of the blows as the crowd roared its delight. They were providing Mad River with another night's entertainment, he thought grimly as he sparred with the big man a moment and then caught a glancing right to his jaw. Red was stopped by the blow for only a second; then he laced into Tim with a furious left to the rib cage and a jab to the side of his head.

The blows were well planted and hurt. Tim reeled slightly, and this gave the circle of onlookers a thirst for a quick kill. They yelled to the outlaw to move in and finish him. But Tim was recovering quickly, and he had a target in the still puffed eye of the big man. As he moved in, he directed a jab to the eye that made Red Barnes stagger back with a cry of pain. Blood spurted from the eye, and Tim knew it would be useless to the big man for the rest of the battle.

When Barnes swooped in on him again, he was in a murderous mood, and the blows he landed on Tim were cruel ones. But not too many landed. The crowd was shouting for more action as the two men in the circle broke apart to move warily. Tim knew what he had to do: either achieve a knockout or close the other eye. After that a knockout would be

70

easy. If he could keep Barnes in a rage, he thought he could manage it.

True to his expectations, Barnes came at him like an angry bull once again. Tim took a couple of nasty body blows but used the opportunity to gain the advantage he'd been waiting for. A vicious jab to the big outlaw's good eye cut it open and left it a pulpy mess. In a minute Red Barnes would be blinded and at his mercy. The big man roared with anger and staggered aimlessly as Tim moved in to finish him. The crowd was hoarse from its delirious shouting.

Tim closed in on the big outlaw and sent a direct uppercut to his chin. It made a loud impact, and Barnes stiffened and then slumped down on the ground. Tim stood over him as he lifted a sleeve to wipe away a smear of blood from his own face. He was not prepared for what followed almost at once.

One of Red's cronies, a swarthy, squat man, darted out from the circle and, roughly grabbing Tim by the arm, swung around to deliver a smashing right to his mouth. Caught by surprise, Tim felt the full force of the blow and fell back a few steps. Bedlam broke out in the circle as the crowd yelled for more blood. Tim ducked a right that barely missed his chin, didn't duck the following left fast enough and went down.

The squat man stood over him with a nasty grin. Instinct made Tim roll as the newcomer tried to jab a boot savagely in his side. Tim didn't give him a second chance. He was on his feet in a second and driving a right and a left at the swarthy man's jaw. Hurt, the swarthy one fell back. Then, with an oath, his right hand stabbed to his gun butt. The gun barrel had cleared leather when Tim's driving boot kicked it a dozen feet away.

Thoroughly aroused now, Tim reached out. His left hand grasped the shirt of the swarthy man and jerked him forward. He hurled his right fist deep into the outlaw's belly. The swarthy man gasped and looked blank. Then he folded and dropped to his knees. Again Tim brought him to his feet, and again he brought his right fist up. It crashed against the swarthy one's jaw, and the shock of it carried all the way up Tim's arm to his shoulder. Somebody in the circle let out a groan. The swarthy man fell sideways to the ground and stayed there.

'The next time you pull a gun like that,' Tim told the unconscious man, 'remember what happened tonight.' He looked around the circle. 'Any others?'

No one answered or made a move. Slowly the anger drained out of Tim. Breathing heavily, he glanced down at the two crumpled figures for a moment, then moved away. He picked up his Stetson, beat it against his leg and put it on his head. Quietly the circle parted to make way for him as he walked toward the entrance of the saloon.

In the privacy of his office, he splashed cold water on his face from a basin in the corner of the room. He'd been lucky enough to escape the struggle with only a few bruises and skinned knuckles.

Back in the saloon, the crowd was thinning out and there were plenty of empty places along the bar. He went up to one and ordered himself a whiskey. He drank it straight and then had another. As the burning liquid coursed down his gullet, he began to feel better.

'I liked the way you handled yourself out there tonight,' a quiet voice said at his elbow.

He turned to see a middle-aged man dressed in sedate gray with a gaunt, lined face. Deep-set, thoughtful eyes studied him from under heavy iron-gray brows. Tim saw at once that this was the face of a responsible, honest man.

He said, 'I was forced into it.'

'I realize that,' the stranger said. 'May I offer you a drink? I know you're the new manager of this place. But I'd still like to treat.'

Tim's smile was thin. 'Being the manager doesn't affect my thirst.'

'Fine,' the stranger said, and ordered drinks for them both. Then he told Tim, 'My name is Lionel Mason. I'm the owner of the Flying K. It's a small ranch north of town.'

Tim eyed him. 'I didn't know there were any small spreads left.'

The stranger sighed. 'There aren't many. My place and a couple of others are the only ones now. And if the Indian raids go on, we won't be able to keep operating.'

Their drinks were served, and Tim lifted his whiskey. 'To the success of the Flying K.'

Lionel Mason's gaunt face brightened. 'I'm glad to drink to that,' he said. And when they'd downed their whiskey, he turned to him and added, 'The sheriff tells me you're starting a new policy here of no liquor for the Indians.'

Tim shrugged. 'Isn't that the law?'

'The Lucky Palomino hasn't been concerned with the law until now,' the rancher said. 'I hope you keep your word.'

'Don't worry about it,' Tim told him.

'It could be the beginning of hope for the smaller ranch owners,' Mason said. 'Without liquor, the Indians may halt their raids.'

'It's a possibility,' Tim agreed. Feeling uncomfortable, he nodded to the rancher and moved on. He wasn't working for the law and didn't want to take any undeserved credit.

He kept to himself until it was time to close the saloon. He didn't see Trent and Flash Moran leave but learned from one of the bartenders that they'd gone out by a rear door. He was becoming more and more unhappy about the position in which he found himself. Gloomily he stood by as the lights were extinguished and the bartenders totaled their proceeds for the night. He remained after everyone else had gone to place the money in a safe in his office. In the morning, he'd take it to the bank.

He'd found himself a room over a restaurant a short distance down the street. It was only a dozen buildings away from the saloon, and so he could walk back and forth. The front entrance was already locked, so he let himself out the rear door and padlocked it after him. Then he made his way along the dark alley to the main street.

From habit he hugged close to the building. As he came out into the street, he thought he saw something move in the shadows of an alley opposite, and the next moment a gun blazed and a bullet whistled by his head. He dropped to the ground and lay still.

CHAPTER SIX

Stretched flat in the middle of the street, Tim reached for his .44 and took aim as two horsemen came out of the alley opposite. He blazed away at them, and they returned his fire. Bullets bit into the ground close to him, and as the riders came near he figured his

75

number was up. But at the critical moment there came the sounds of an approaching rider, and the other two took fright and galloped off, after firing at him for a last time. The final bullet seared his shoulder and brought him burning pain.

The intruder on the violent scene came close as Tim got to his feet. The rider reined the mount short and, leaning over the saddle, asked, 'What kind of trouble are you in now?' It was the pleasant female voice of Sheriff Susan Slade.

'The same battle,' he said with a wry grin. 'It just seems go keep going on. I reckon that was Red Barnes or some of his cronies.'

Susan Slade stared down at him. 'I hear you two had another set-to in the street.'

'He insisted on it.'

'You're in bad trouble in this town,' she told him. 'I suppose you know that.'

'I've been in bad trouble for a long while. I'm used to it.'

'You're lucky you didn't get plugged just now. Where are you heading?'

'Not far. Just a couple of houses down. I've a room over Julie's eating place.'

'I'll see you safely there,' she said.

'No need.'

'There seems to be,' she said with irony. And loosening the reins, she let her horse move on as he walked alongside.

He asked, 'Do you usually patrol the

streets alone at this late hour?'

'Don't you consider it safe for a female, even a female sheriff?' Her tone was mocking.

'I admit I can't get used to the idea,' he confessed.

'Wearing a star gives a person pretty good protection,' she told him.

'It can also make you a target,' he reminded her.

They had come to the restaurant building and the wooden steps at the side that led to the second level where he had his room. She brought her horse to a halt again.

'I'm not worried,' she told him. 'The outlaw crowd here want me as sheriff. They figure it makes it that much safer for them. I know they're laughing at me, but I'm biding my time till I get the last laugh.'

He smiled up at her. 'I hope you get it.'

'I think I will,' she said. 'You still feel working for Trent is a good idea?'

'It will do for a little.'

She shook her head. 'Sometimes I think you're pretty sensible, and then you spoil it all.' And with that she rode on down the street in the direction of the jailhouse.

The stinging pain in his shoulder reminded Tim that he had been wounded in the brief fray in the street. He mounted the outside steps to the second floor of the restaurant building and went down the narrow hallway to his room. The walls of the building were

77

far from soundproof, and the snores of the occupants of the other rooms shattered the stillness of the night. He went inside and, lighting the single lamp provided, began to investigate his wound by the feeble light penetrating the murky lampshade.

It turned out to be a surface welt, a little deeper than was comfortable. He washed it in clean cold water and put a temporary bandage over it. Because it was his right shoulder, he'd have a stiff gun arm in the morning. He hoped the running feud with Red Barnes and his outlaw cronies had come to an end, but he couldn't be certain.

Next morning when Tim took the cash over to the bank, he was called into the private office of Neil Neilson. The three-hundred-pound banker sat behind his desk with a disconsolate expression on his pink baby-face. The resemblance to an overweight infant was emphasized by his baldness.

Waving Tim to an empty chair before the desk, he addressed him in his high-pitched voice. 'I hear you were mixed up in a street battle last night, Parker.'

Tim nodded grimly. 'That's right.'

'You must avoid such fights if you're going to continue working for us,' the banker warned him. 'We want things to go smoothly at the Lucky Palomino.'

Tim eyed the huge, pink-cheeked man with

78

barely disguised contempt. 'You want your dirty work to look clean.'

Neil Neilson frowned. 'I'd advise you to keep a civil tongue, Mr. Parker,' he fussed. 'We have hired you for your particular skill with a gun, not to criticize us or engage in brawls with the town bully.'

'Since I suspect the town bully is also working for your group, you might pass that information along to him,' Tim suggested.

'Barnes has gotten out of hand,' the banker agreed primly. 'Trent is going to reprimand him.'

'About time,' Tim said dryly. 'And while he's about it, he might speak to Flash Moran as well, since he's the one who put Barnes up to starting a fight with me.'

The fat banker showed no expression. 'Moran is a good man, even if he does make a mistake now and then.'

'Meaning he's more valuable to you than Barnes,' Tim said with some bitterness.

Neil Neilson clasped his small hands on his ample stomach and studied Tim gloomily. 'Frankness is never a social asset, Parker,' he said in his squeaky voice.

'I'll try to remember that.'

'I hear you have a funny thing about redskins.'

Tim's face went stern. 'I don't like them around.'

'So Trent tells me,' the banker went on,

watching him with his tiny pale blue eyes. 'Well, maybe you'll get over that.'

'I wouldn't count on it,' Tim said, rising. 'Anything else you want to tell me? I should be getting back to the Lucky Palomino.'

The fat man sighed. 'You're a very impulsive type. You should curb that. About that redskin business: a good many people around here hate them. The Indians have done a lot of damage to the ranches in the district. The bank has had to take over a number of spreads from people who figure it isn't worth battling against raids any longer.'

Tim gave him a hard smile. 'Does that make you sad? I hear the Union Pacific's coming along any day now to buy a right-of-way through a lot of those ranches.'

Neil Neilson's chubby pink face showed concern. 'Frankness again, Parker,' he warned him.

Tim left the bank with a feeling of relief. He liked none of the trio who had hired him. And he found the chubby banker the most disgusting of them all.

Before Tim could mount the mare, a rider came down the street, trailing a cloud of dust. As he came close Tim saw that it was Deputy Pete Holm. The grizzled lawman reined his horse and glared down at him.

'Sheriff wants you,' he said.

Tim frowned. 'Isn't this getting to be a habit?'

80

'No time for jokes,' the old man with the deputy's star said. 'She wants you at the jailhouse pronto, and she's got a good reason.'

'I'll stop by,' Tim agreed.

'I'll ride along with you,' Deputy Pete Holm said with meaning.

Tim stared at him. 'You taking me in?'

'I wouldn't call it that,' the old lawman said, but the look on his weary face was stern.

Tim swung into the saddle and headed the piebald mare around. 'Seems to me the law is giving me a lot of attention,' he said. 'Don't you have any other customers?'

Deputy Pete Holm looked straight ahead. 'You attract more than your fair share of trouble.'

They rode the rest of the way to the jailhouse in silence.

When Tim and Deputy Holm entered the small office with its worn plank floor and the parcel of wanted posters on its rear wall, there was no one in sight. The old deputy gave Tim a grim glance and left him to go out back. A few minutes later, while he was standing reading a poster about a killer wanted by the authorities in Arizona and Texas, he heard someone coming into the office. He turned and saw it was Susan Slade. The girl sheriff had an angry look on her attractive face.

'How long do you suppose it will be before you rate a poster like that?' she asked him.

He managed a feeble smile. 'First time I've

81

ever been accused of being a killer.'

Her eyes angrily challenged him. 'Your gun is for hire.'

'I won't deny that.'

'Not much use doing it when I know Trent owns you.'

Tim frowned. 'I don't like that word "owns".'

'It tells the story.'

'Not the true one,' he said. 'I'm managing the Lucky Palomino for Trent, and that's only a limited deal. Nobody owns me.'

The girl sheriff shook her head. 'How can you be so stupid?' she wanted to know. 'Every last man who hires out his gun to the highest bidder, like you've been doing, winds up a killer with a price on his head.'

'I haven't thought much about it,' he said with pretended casualness.

The girl gave him a despairing glance. 'I wish you would,' she said. 'When I first met you, I thought you were a cut above the average saddle tramp come into town for a quick and easy dollar. Now I'm wondering.'

'Wondering about what?'

'You're pretty fed up with Red Barnes.'

'I guess I am.'

Susan Slade's eyes met his. 'And I guess Trent doesn't much like your battling with that outlaw. Squabbles in the family don't pay off.'

'I don't claim any kinship with Barnes.'

'You're kin just the same,' she said evenly. 'Barnes played Trent's games long before you ever showed up in Mad River.'

'I wouldn't know about that.'

Her smile was sour. 'You make a habit of not knowing about anything that might bother you.'

'That's normal.'

'I guess it is, she said. 'Where did you go after I left you last night?'

'To my room. You must have seen me go upstairs before you rode away.'

'I didn't wait,' she said. 'Did you go back out again and look for Red Barnes?'

'Not likely,' he said. 'I took care of my wounded shoulder. Barnes or one of his loco friends drilled me.' He indicated his right shoulder. 'It's nice and sore today.'

'I see,' she said. 'So your story is that you went to your room and stayed there?'

'That's it. Why all the questions?'

She stared at him in silence for a moment, a strange expression on her pretty face. Then she said, 'Come out back. I want to show you something.'

She led the way down a short dark hall. Continuing out the back, she came to a sort of shed. Throwing open a wooden door, she stood to one side.

'Take a look in there,' she suggested.

He stared at her drawn, angry face and with a shrug stepped into the shadowy room.

83

It took a minute for his eyes to adjust; and then he saw the body on its back on the plank floor. It was the body of Red Barnes, and there was a messy hole in the middle of his forehead where a bullet had crashed through the bone. The big man's face wore a startled look. Death had come swiftly and unexpectedly.

Tim turned and emerged from the shed, feeling a little sick. The girl sheriff was waiting there for him, carefully noting his reaction to what he'd just seen. Now he understood the mystery behind his summons to the jailhouse.

She said, 'So that settles Mr.. Red Barnes.'

'I guess it does,' he said tautly.

'And I can't think of anyone with better reason to plant that bullet in his skull than you,' she said sternly.

'It wasn't me.'

'Maybe not,' she agreed. 'But I reckon it must have been done on account of you.'

He gave her an uneasy glance. 'I want you to know I didn't have any part in this.'

'You work for Trent.'

'What if I do?'

'This is the kind of thing Trent makes happen. By working for him, you're giving it your stamp of approval.'

He said, 'Life can do things to a man. A time comes when you've got loyalty to no one but yourself.'

Her smile was grim. 'I don't think a human can live that way. Not a decent one.'

'You can be tolerant,' he said. 'You haven't suffered much.'

The girl's eyes flashed angrily. 'I lost my mother to a fever when I was too young to remember her. And I saw my father shot down!'

His eyes met hers. 'My wife was murdered by a skulking half-breed, and the law wouldn't do anything about it.'

'Is that it? Is that why you became what you are?'

He shrugged, wondering why he was telling her all this. He'd never mentioned it to anyone before. 'My gun wasn't for hire until that happened.'

Susan Slade's attractive face showed compassion. 'I can understand it was a hard blow. But was it reason enough to turn renegade, to hate all Indians? Are you entitled to that much self-pity?'

'I wouldn't call it that,' he said defensively.

'I would,' she insisted. 'At least I've stayed here and faced up to reality. I may have given some people in town the idea they're using me. But I took this sheriff's job for a reason: to carry on the work my father began.'

'Do you expect to have any luck with it?'

'I can try,' she said. 'At least I haven't given up, as you have.'

He studied her for a long moment. 'The

85

lecture over?'

'Yes. I wanted you to come here and see Barnes, see what all this leads to. I'll be sending him to the undertaker's shortly. If you're wise, you'll get out of town right away. Stay on here with Trent, and you'll wind up with a bullet in your head like Barnes or with your name on one of those wanted posters like the one in my office.'

Tim smiled thinly. 'I don't aim to do either. I'm going to play it real cool.'

The girl looked sad. 'Don't say you weren't warned.'

'I won't,' he said. And with a nod he left her.

CHAPTER SEVEN

When Tim bearded the mayor of Mad River in the office of his hardware store, the florid-faced, dark man pretended small interest in Red's death. Tim knew it was a pretense, yet he hesitated to face a showdown. Something told him this was the wrong time. But he did speak of his continuing trouble with Flash Moran. The gambler was operating entirely on his own and offering Tim sneering bravado whenever he attempted to make Flash keep in line.

Jim Trent listened sullenly as Tim pointed

86

out that the gambler was deliberately bucking him. The mayor waited until he'd finished and then, staring at the worn carpet on his office floor and carefully avoiding Tim's eyes, observed, 'Seems to me you're a mite too sensitive about Moran and what he says or does.'

Tim stood there angrily. 'I don't trust him. He caused the trouble with Red Barnes, and he's giving me all the headaches he can now.'

'Barnes was a fool and a bully. You shouldn't blame Moran for the way he acted.'

'I saw Moran put him up to baiting me,' Tim protested.

The mayor continued to study the drab carpet. 'It would be best if you forgot all about that,' he said.

'I'm not sure I can go on running the saloon with him there.'

Trent frowned. 'We need Moran at the table. He's bringing in a good profit.'

Tim rested a hand on the butt of his .44. 'It may come to your deciding who you need more—him or me.'

'I hope not,' Trent said enigmatically.

And Tim left it there. But he wasn't happy. Flash Moran stayed out of his way after the conversation with Trent, but Tim knew the gambler was still working against him. And sooner or later there was bound to be an explosion between them.

In the weeks that followed there were no

raids on the small ranchers. And things had quietened down in Mad River itself. It was as if the killing of Red Barnes had put an end to most of the violence in the district. Yet Tim had an uneasy suspicion this was just a lull between storms. There was a vicious element present in the cow town, and every night he saw a lot of them at the tables and the bar of the Lucky Palomino.

Tim tried to turn his back on the growing signs of a gathering storm. Tension hovered in the air like the heat that rose from the dusty streets. There were rumors that the Indians were gathering in the hills for another series of raids. And he heard stories that several of the small ranch owners weren't going to wait for the raids to become a reality, but were already negotiating to sell out to the syndicate headed by Jim Trent. It was significant that the Sioux never seemed to hit any of the syndicate's holdings.

A rangy Swede by the name of Olsen did sell out and move on to more friendly frontier country. Then Tim was surprised to hear that Lionel Mason, the quiet rancher with the gaunt face, was about to get rid of his spread. He couldn't understand this, because Mason had struck him as a fighter. It wasn't like the rancher to give up before he'd suffered a redskin attack. And when Mason appeared in the Lucky Palomino a few nights later, Tim approached him about the matter.

Inviting the rancher into his office, he asked him, 'What's this I hear about you selling the Flying K and getting out?'

The rancher's lean face showed a grim smile. 'I reckon that's wishful thinking on some folks' part,' he said.

'Then you aren't leaving?'

'Not unless they force me out,' was Lionel Mason's firm reply. 'There's a lot of whispering about coming raids. And there are only a few of us independents left, so it's hard to say what will happen.'

'Have you talked to the sheriff about protection?'

Mason nodded. 'Yes. And she's promised to do what she can. Deputy Holm is going to police my range every few nights or so to scare any prospective raiders off.'

Tim said, 'That sounds like the first constructive move that's been made against the Sioux yet.'

'I'd say it is.'

'Maybe they'll leave you alone.'

'I don't count on it,' Mason said. 'All my neighbors have had their turn. It makes a man pretty edgy to know what may happen any night. But I've got all I ever worked for tied up in my ranch.'

'I hope things turn out better than you think,' Tim said.

The rancher's gaunt face had a strange expression. 'I can't figure why you should be on my side, since you work for Trent.'

'Why not?'

'You know how most of us feel about Mayor Trent,' the other man said with disgust. 'And by the way, are you keeping up your policy of no liquor to the Indians?'

'Yes.'

'I don't think it's working very well,' Mason told him. 'They're getting booze just the same, and I've heard it's coming from here.'

'Not that I know,' Tim insisted, his anger rising at the thought that someone in the saloon might be guilty of a double-cross.

Mason looked wise. 'I'd keep a sharp eye out,' he said. 'That is, if you're really serious in what you said.'

'I am serious,' Tim assured him.

After the rancher left, he had a talk with the sullen barkeep, Herbie. The big head man insisted that no one had given the Sioux any liquor. But Tim thought his protests shifty and evasive. He didn't bother to question Flash Moran, knowing he'd get nothing but arrogant denials. But he did make up his mind to keep a closer watch on the gambler's activities. He had an idea it might pay off.

Shortly afterward, Preacher Abel Gray came by the Lucky Palomino one evening. It was early, before the saloon had really filled up. He smiled at Tim and said, 'We haven't seen anything of you lately.'

Tim was embarrassed. He'd been deliberately trying to keep out of the way of the preacher and his daughter. He said, 'I've been tied up here.'

The middle-aged man in the neat dark suit and clerical collar gazed about the large room. He sighed. 'It's strange that you can fill this place every night, and I can't manage to get even a fair-sized group in my small church.'

Tim smiled ruefully. 'I think I warned you, Reverend. The prospects for a church in Mad River aren't good.'

The older man looked resigned. 'I'm not going to give up, I promise you that. But it is disappointing.'

'I'm sorry.'

The Reverend Abel Gray changed the subject, 'I've come here for a purpose,' he said. 'My daughter is having a special meal for me tomorrow night, since it happens to be my birthday. And we'd both like you to join us.'

Tim hesitated. 'It isn't easy to get away from here.'

'I know that. But we can have dinner early. Your crowd here doesn't start until fairly late in the evening.'

This was true. Tim decided to accept the invitation and stay only a little while.

'I guess I can join you,' he said. 'But I'll have to leave early.'

91

The preacher looked pleased. 'Sabrina and I understand that. You'll find her an excellent cook. We're to have chicken, which is a favorite dish with me when roasted Maryland style as Sabrina does it. Shall we say six sharp?'

'I'll be there,' Tim agreed.

The next evening, Sabrina greeted him in a pretty pale green dress that suited her soft blonde beauty. And the meal was a triumph. Tim was impressed by what her womanly touch had done to the drab back rooms of the store. Dainty curtains at the windows and new wallpaper gave it her personal touch.

The store in front had also been newly decorated as a chapel. Its whitewashed walls and the pulpit gave it a different appearance. Sabrina and her father took Tim out to see it after they had finished the excellent birthday dinner.

Standing by the pulpit, the preacher said, 'I'm pleased to say we have managed to reach out to a few of the local Indians. And we've found them not such a bad lot.'

'I'm glad,' Tim said stiffly. It was something he didn't want to discuss.

Sabrina gave him a reproachful smile. 'I know you're prejudiced. But the ones who have shown up here have been rather forlorn. They complain of being cheated in the local stores and given bad treatment generally, but they are meek enough about it.'

The Reverend Abel Gray addressed himself to Tim. 'They're still getting liquor, you know.'

'So I've heard,' Tim acknowledged. 'I can promise it's not through me.'

The older man nodded approval. 'I'm glad to hear that.' A few moments later he excused himself to call on one of his ailing flock, and Sabrina and Tim were left alone together.

They returned to the comfortable big room behind the chapel. Seating herself on a love seat, Sabrina asked him, 'Do you still think you're in the right job?'

He shrugged. 'It's a job I know.'

'But you were a rancher once,' she pointed out.

'I was once.'

'Don't you ever think of returning to that life again?'

Tim shook his head. 'Never.'

'I see,' she said, her hands clasped in her lap. She studied them with a sad expression.

He stood there in awkward silence for a long moment. Then he said, 'It's hard for a man to go back over his life and start again. What it amounts to is that you're no longer the same man you once were.'

The blonde girl looked up at him anxiously. 'I'm afraid for you, Tim.'

Her use of his first name and the tone in which she spoke combined to startle him. He asked, 'Why?'

'You must know as well as I do. There's going to be terrible trouble breaking out here soon. Everybody says so, and that girl sheriff isn't going to be able to cope with it. Dad thinks she is kept in her job thanks to outlaw support.'

Tim frowned at this outburst. 'If trouble comes, everyone is in danger. And your Dad is wrong about Susan Slade. She wants to be a good sheriff.'

Sabrina protested, 'But she's just a girl like me!'

'Not exactly. Her Dad was the sheriff before her, and she grew up around the law, knowing what it meant to be a law officer. And she's got a good deputy to help her.'

The blonde girl stood up and stared at him. 'You talk as if you really believe her capable of keeping law and order here.'

'She's not doing a bad job.'

Her blue eyes searched his face. 'Are you in love with her, Tim?'

Her abrupt question came as another shock. He lifted his eyebrows. 'Why do you ask that?'

'I don't know,' she said helplessly. 'The way you talk about her suggests she truly means something to you.'

He swallowed hard. 'I think she deserves credit.'

'I see,' Sabrina said quietly.

'And I say your Dad is wrong in thinking

she's in with the crooked element in town.'

Sabrina seemed strangely subdued. 'I'll tell him what you said,' she promised.

Tim eyed her with concern. 'The two people I calculate will be least able to survive if trouble strikes Mad River are you and your Dad.'

The blonde girl crimsoned. 'We're not so stupid or weak as you seem to believe, Mr. Parker!'

He smiled dourly. 'It's Mr. Parker now, is it?'

'I don't think you should treat us with scorn because we are trying to do some good in the town,' she said, apparently near tears.

'You're wrong about that. I'm not scornful of you,' he said solemnly, taking her by the arms. 'But I know it's decent people of your type who always get hurt first.'

Her eyes met his, and tears sprang from them. 'I am terribly frightened, Tim—for Dad, for you, for all of us!'

Impulsively he drew her close and kissed her. After he realized what had happened, he let her go.

'I'm sorry,' he apologized. 'I had no right to do that.'

Her eyes were tender. 'You have every right, if that's what you wanted to do.'

Tim frowned. 'You don't understand!'

Sabrina sighed. 'I understand only too well. You can't bar every bit of love from your life,

Tim. That's what you've tried to do, and see where it has led you—working as a saloon boss and hired gunman for somebody like Trent!'

'My business,' he warned her.

'You can't have been hurt that badly,' Sabrina protested. 'Don't tell me your wife would have wanted you to become the kind of person you are now! You can't continue to live with all this pent-up hatred without destroying yourself.'

Tim smiled thinly. 'I thought the sermons would be confined to your chapel.'

'Tim!' the blonde girl said in reproach, blushing furiously once more.

'It was a nice dinner, Sabrina,' he said. 'Wish your Dad a happy birthday again for me.' And he turned and stalked out of the little room without looking back.

He marched across the street. And as he went up the wooden sidewalk toward the lights and revelry of the Lucky Palomino, he continued to scowl. Pushing his way through the swing doors, he saw the saloon was crowded. Staring down its smoke-filled length he was startled to see no sign of Flash Moran. There was no game going on.

Amazed at this, he turned his eyes toward the bar. Far in the back the head bartender, Herbie, was standing watching him nervously. Tim could tell by the attitude of the hulking man that something was going on.

CHAPTER EIGHT

Tim went directly to Herbie and asked him where Flash Moran was. The big man pretended not to have noticed Moran was away from his table. Impatiently leaving the bartender, Tim pushed his way through the crowded room to the door leading to the rear of the building. He opened it and went down the long, narrow, dark passage to the large storage area in the back.

He thought he heard subdued voices and movement ahead in the darkness. Drawing his .44 from its holster, he went forward stealthily. A creaking board underfoot gave him a start, and he continued slowly. As his eyes became accustomed to the shadows, he saw the crouched form of a man on the edge of the back platform, passing something to somebody on the ground.

Increasing his pace, he moved in on the scene in time to catch Flash Moran handing what was apparently the last of several bottles to the half-breed, Wolf. Tim didn't hesitate but pressed the trigger of the .44. The bullet blazed out in the darkness and splintered the bottle while it was still in Flash Moran's hand.

With a cry of alarm, the squat man wheeled

around and, finding his own gun, returned the fire. Tim neatly dodged the bullet and sprang forward to grasp the gambler and wrest the gun from his hand. The struggle between them began as the renegade Wolf and his comrades scurried off into the night. Moran cursed fiercely and put up a surprisingly agile resistance. But Tim was a younger and stronger man.

Once he'd disposed of the gambler's gun, Tim gave the stout man a sound beating that brought him whimpering and gasping to his knees. Though they were still in darkness, he was sure the gambler knew who his opponent was. This was borne out when Moran began to beg for pity.

'Stop it, Parker!' he pleaded. 'I've had enough!'

Tim stood over him with his .44 in his hand again. In a cold voice, he said, 'So you went right on with your liquor traffic to the Sioux!'

'It wasn't me, Parker; it was Trent's orders,' the battered Moran protested. All the fight had gone out of him.

Tim listened stolidly. He didn't doubt the gambler was telling him the truth, yet he knew that Moran had also prospered in the dirty trade. And it had been Moran who'd delighted in crossing him to carry out Trent's instructions.

In a tone of disgust, he said, 'All right. Get

on your feet. And don't try to find your gun.'

'Sure, Parker.' The gambler laboriously got up from his knees and stood before him.

'And don't try any tricks like setting one of your thug friends against me,' Tim warned him. 'I've just about lost my patience with you.'

'I won't give you no more trouble,' the beaten wretch sniveled. 'I promise that.'

'What's a promise of yours worth?' Tim demanded in disgust. And he turned away from the gambler and started along the shadowy hall leading to the saloon.

He was in a state of rage. As he'd suspected, Trent had paid no attention to his demand that the Indians not be sold liquor. Instead, the wily mayor had put Flash Moran in charge of that part of the operation. The alcohol had been getting to the redskins as usual. It meant only one thing. He was finished as Trent's henchman. He was going to confront the crooked political leader and tell him so. In a way, he was glad of an excuse.

Not halting to speak to anyone in the saloon, he made his way directly to the hardware store. As usual at this time of night, the front door was locked. Peering in the window, he could see a dim light from Trent's private office in the rear. He went around by the alley and found the back door.

Then he pounded on it.

In several minutes there were shuffling footsteps in the corridor. Then a wary voice questioned through the door, 'Who is it?' It was Trent.

Tim said, 'It's Parker, and I want to talk to you pronto.'

There was the sound of a bolt being slid back, and then the door was slowly opened. Trent peered out at Tim and in a tone of rebuke told him, 'You should be back at the saloon. It's the peak business time.'

'We'll talk about that,' Tim said, edging his way inside.

'I hope this is important,' Trent said as he bolted the door again. 'Neilson and the judge are here discussing business with me, and they don't much like being interrupted.'

'I've got a good reason,' Tim said curtly.

'We'll see about that,' the dark-haired mayor said. But he led Tim to his private office.

Tim mounted the few steps to the office level and found himself in the dingy, lamp-lit room facing the obnoxious trio.

In his whining voice the judge told him, 'You're supposed to be at the Lucky Palomino right now taking care of our interests!'

Jim Trent had slumped down in his swivel chair before the roll-top desk. With a disgusted expression on his hard face, he said,

'I've told him that.'

Fat Neilson leaned forward in his chair to add, 'Well, I don't see that it hurts to say it again.'

'Well, Parker,' Trent said, 'what's biting you?'

Tim's eyes were fixed on the mayor. 'I've just come from having an interesting chat with Flash Moran.'

Trent laughed harshly. 'First time I ever heard anyone call Moran interesting.'

Tim's eyes narrowed. 'It's what he said that struck me,' he told the dark man. 'According to him, he was selling booze to Wolf and the rest of the Indians on your orders.'

The man in the swivel chair didn't answer right away. Instead, he gave the fat Neilson and the squinting judge a significant glance. 'I suppose we had to look for something like this,' he told them.

The judge snapped, 'Since when does it take you to tell us how to run our business?'

'That's what I say,' Banker Neilson piped up in his squeaky voice.

Tim gazed at the trio with contempt. 'When I took over the running of the Lucky Palomino, I told you there was to be no trade with the Sioux! And I meant it.'

Jim Trent raised a placating hand. 'We know you've got a bee in your bonnet about Injuns and liquor,' he said. 'And we've been ready to go along with it. That's why we told

101

Moran to handle any trade of that kind on the side and not disturb you.'

Tim snapped, 'You told him to go ahead behind my back.'

Jim Trent rose up from his chair, his coarse face livid with rage. 'We've got serious problems to consider and no time to put up with you barging in here with a lot of fool complaints.'

Tim stared at him. 'You expect me to accept this?'

Trent nodded. 'I sure enough do. Who do you think you are, Parker? And if you don't know, I'll tell you who and what you are! You're a saddle tramp we hired and brought here to do what we asked!'

'That's right,' the fat banker echoed. 'You're just another hired gun, and we don't aim to be bothered by your views.'

'Trash should keep their place,' the judge said querulously. 'It's your fault, Trent, for ever lettin' this renegade meet us!'

In a way, Tim knew they were right. When a man hired out his gun and his principles, he didn't reserve any right to question what he was ordered to do.

Mistaking his silence for agreement, Trent addressed him in a friendlier tone. 'I suggest we forget all about this, Parker. You go back to your job, and we'll get down to our business. You look after the saloon, and don't interfere with Moran. I reckon you can still work together. Your argument didn't go that far?' This last was a question, put hopefully.

It gave Tim satisfaction to smile grimly and inform them, 'We had quite a battle, gents. He isn't going to look pretty for a spell.'

Trent frowned. 'That's too bad. Flash has a nasty temper. He won't let it go at that. It complicates things.'

'Oh, it won't do that,' Tim said wisely. 'The fact is, gentlemen, I'm not working for you any longer.'

Trent frowned. 'You can't quit. We paid you a good advance.'

'Too much!' the fat banker said indignantly.

'No better than stealing!' was the querulous comment of the scrawny old judge.

'Just the same, I'm through,' Tim told the trio.

The mayor was staring at him with hatred in his eyes. 'If that's the way you want it, Parker,' he said. 'Maybe you're right after all. I'm not sure you're going to be of much more use to us. But I warn you: get out of Mad River. From now on this town isn't going to be healthy for you.'

Tim's tanned face wore a derisive look. 'It doesn't happen to be my favorite spot.'

'Just get out, that's all I ask,' Jim Trent said with controlled rage. 'And don't think this won't cost you plenty. I'm seeing the word spreads that you're a welsher. You may not find your next job so easy to come by.'

'I'm not worried,' Tim told him, 'just as long as I'm free of this mess.'

He kept his hand on the Colt .44 as he backed out of the office and left the three staring after him in anger. Then he quickly made his way to the rear of the store again, slipped the bolt of the back door and hurried out into the cool darkness. He'd only gone three or four steps before he heard a stirring in the pitch blackness behind him. And the next instant he was pounced on by a massive and powerful adversary. He drew his gun, but it was kicked from his hand almost as he touched it. And then the massive hands gripped his throat and tightened until gradually the breath was choked out of him.

A harsh laugh and a snarled, 'Not so smart this time!' told him it was the giant bartender, Herbie, whom Moran had sent after him.

Trying to keep his mind clear, Tim marshaled his strength and kicked out in the region of the giant's groin as hard as he could. The big man roared with anger and pain. At the same time he relaxed his hold on Tim's throat just a little. But it was enough. Flailing at the giant with his fists, Tim managed to escape from the killer's hands and stumble back into the darkness of the alley.

The big man bore down on him again, but this time Tim was not caught by surprise. He dodged back and then came darting forward to pummel the mammoth Herbie about the face. The quick rain of blows was telling, and the big man did not manage to punish Tim much in return. Tim was gradually recovering from the first terrible punishment he'd received and was now careful to keep out of the giant's grasp. His best chance was to move in and deliver a telling blow or two, and nimbly get out of Herbie's reach.

The bartender fought more savagely as he began to take severe punishment. But his wild blows were largely misdirected. After a long period of scuffling and battling in the darkness, Tim landed a right to Herbie's chin that sent him slumping to his knees with a light moan. Tim quickly followed with a rain of lefts and rights to the face and head. It was the end as far as the giant was concerned. He fell sideways and stayed motionless on the hard ground.

Breathing heavily, Tim lit a match and found his .44 and hat. Then he got out of the alley as quickly as he could, leaving the unconscious Herbie behind him. He could see that Mad River would be a tough place to survive in, and he hadn't any desire to remain there much longer. But there were a few things he wanted to settle before he left.

He made his way to the livery stable and had the mare saddled. Then he swung up in the saddle and began the ride out to Sam

Smith's desert castle.

A sleepy Indian servant admitted him, and he decided not to disturb Smith.

In the morning, he washed and went downstairs. The great house seemed empty and deserted, and he began to wonder if his host had gone off somewhere.

Then the old prospector surprised him by appearing from a rear hallway of the house.

'Glad to see you,' the prospector greeted him. 'But what about your job?'

'I'm a free man,' Tim said. 'Last night I walked out on Trent and the Lucky Palomino.'

Sam Smith whistled low. 'Now I expect that didn't please Trent and his partners a mite.'

'They were pretty upset.'

'Trent is a bad enemy to have in this town,' the old prospector warned him.

'I know.'

'But you decided not to tote a gun for him any more no matter what?'

'That's about it,' Tim said, his handsome face serious. 'I caught Flash Moran feeding the redskins whiskey. I guess he's been doing that ever since I came and refused to have anything to do with the trade.'

'So that's what made you quit?'

'I wanted an excuse anyhow,' Tim admitted. 'And this gave me a good one.'

'What did Trent say?'

106

'That Mad River wasn't going to be too healthy for me.'

'He's right,' the old man agreed, nodding solemnly. 'Your life won't be worth a plugged nickel if you stay around.'

'I've managed pretty well so far,' Tim reminded him.

The wizened Sam Smith shook his head. 'You don't know the power those men have. You're no match for them and their killers.'

'I was one of their hired guns myself. Remember?'

'Sure,' the grizzled prospector said. 'But you're on the outside now, and alone. You should lie low for a spell. You're welcome to stay here. Can you play checkers?'

'A little.'

'Great,' the old man said enthusiastically. 'I've been looking for a partner to play with. You can stay here as long as you like.'

Tim shook his head. 'Thanks, but I'm moving on.'

The prospector looked forlorn. 'I figured when you came out here you wanted to see me about something.'

'I did. I wanted to say goodbye. You were one of the first people I met on the stage. It seemed right you should be one of the last I talk with before I leave.'

The wizened little man looked flattered. 'That's right nice of you, son. I only wish you'd stay. A man gets lonely out here in this

107

big place.'

'I can imagine,' Tim said. 'Maybe I'll come back this way sometime and will settle down here with you for a spell.'

'Wish you'd promise me that,' Sam Smith told him.

'Now I'm heading back to town to see some other people,' Tim said.

The old man gave him a sly wink. 'I'm thinking one of them will be that pretty little blonde girl who was on the stage.'

Tim smiled. 'You're right. I do want to say goodbye to Sabrina and her Dad. They're fine people. Mad River is lucky to have them there.'

Sam Smith nodded. 'Yep. I reckon so. But I don't expect the reverend to last long. He's bound to give up on a lawless burg like Trent is running.'

'If the decent people banded together, they could vote Trent out and make it a respectable town.'

The little man stroked his short black beard. 'Nary a soul would dare run against him, except perhaps me. And they wouldn't vote for me because they figure I'm loco.'

Tim chuckled. 'Maybe a loco mayor is what Mad River needs.'

'I'm goin' to ride into town with you,' Sam Smith announced. 'I'm plumb weary of wanderin' around here talkin' to myself and having those Injuns of mine starin' at me.'

'Come along if you like,' Tim said. 'But I could be dangerous company if Trent decides to start gunning for me.'

'I'll risk that,' the old man said dryly. 'Matter of fact, I'm still pretty fast on the trigger myself.' And he drew a six-gun from his belt to prove it.

Tim was impressed. 'Very neat,' he said.

They made a strange pair as they rode into town together. The old prospector was mounted on a burro and trailed behind Tim on the mare. The dust rolled up between them, so that every once in a while Tim lost sight of the old man altogether. They arrived in Mad River just before noon, and the town seemed quiet enough. Tim headed straight for the store where the Reverend Gray had set up his church.

He'd tied his mare to a nearby hitching post and was walking along the wooden sidewalk to go into the whitewashed room which the reverend had designated as his chapel before Sam Smith came riding up on the burro. The old man waved and shouted something about joining him.

Tim waved back and nodded in agreement. Then he opened the door and went into the store serving as a mission. There was no one in the room with the pulpit. He was about to cross the door leading to the living quarters in the back when it opened and Preacher Abel Gray came out.

He showed surprise on seeing Tim. 'I didn't expect to see you so early in the day,' he said.

'I reckon not.' Tim smiled. 'But this is a kind of special occasion.'

The preacher showed concern. 'I agree it is,' he said. 'What a terrible thing that the raids have started again.'

'The raids?'

The older man nodded. 'Surely you've heard?'

Tim was stunned. 'No. I haven't heard. Where was the raid?'

'The Indians hit Lionel Mason's ranch last night,' the preacher told him.

CHAPTER NINE

Tim asked the preacher, 'Was there much damage done?'

'Not as much as there could have been,' the older man said. 'The raiders burned down a few of the outbuildings and got away with some cattle. But the ranch and most of the stock were saved.'

'Is Mason safe?'

'Yes.' Preacher Abel Gray nodded. 'We can be thankful for that. He's a fine man. But the town lost one good servant last night. Deputy Pete Holm was at the ranch with some of his

110

men, and he was cut down in the gun battle.'

Consternation crossed Tim's tanned features. 'They killed poor old Pete?'

'Yes. He was there when the raid took place. It was thanks to him and his men that things weren't worse.'

At this point old Sam Smith came in to join them, and Tim told him the news. The veteran prospector looked upset. 'Same old trouble stirring,' he said. 'Do you know my Injuns at the house were actin' kind of funny last night. They always do when a raid is about to happen. I reckon they pass the word along even to my housebroken specimens.'

Tim's face was stern. 'I think you're only imagining that. I doubt if many Indians were involved in the raid. Maybe Wolf and a few of his drunken friends. They're just used as window dressing to cover up for the renegades Trent and his men hire.'

'I agree,' Preacher Abel Gray said. 'The Indians who do get drunk in town are encouraged by the worst element of white men.'

The wizened prospector gave them a dubious look. 'You may think that, and you may even be right. But you'll have a hard time provin' it.'

'I realize the unfair prejudice against red men only too well,' the clergyman said sadly.

The old prospector gave Tim a sly grin and said, 'Even our young friend here don't like

111

the varmints. He claimed the ones at my castle made him jittery when he was out there.'

Tim found himself in an embarrassing position. 'I don't want any part of Indians,' he admitted. 'But I still don't want to see Trent and his crooked crowd get away with blaming those raids on them.'

'Then why do you stay on at the Lucky Palomino where the Indians get their liquor?' It was a defiant Sabrina who asked this of him. The pretty blonde girl had come to stand in the doorway.

He looked at her. 'I'm not at the saloon any longer. I quit last night, before the raid.'

The preacher's daughter brightened as she came over to him. 'Tim, how wonderful! I knew you'd eventually break away from that kind of life.'

He eyed her cynically. 'I didn't say I'd reformed,' he warned her. 'I just told you I'd quit working for Trent.'

Behind her, Preacher Abel Gray smiled. 'I'd say that's good enough for a start.'

'Maybe enough to get him drilled by a bullet from one of Trent's men,' Sam Smith said.

Sabrina gave the old prospector a frightened glance. 'You're right, Mr. Smith.' And to Tim she added, 'You should get out of town at once.'

'I was ready to leave,' he admitted. 'I don't

know now.'

'You must go,' she implored him.

'It's the wise thing,' Sam Smith agreed from the sidelines.

Preacher Abel Gray took a more practical approach. 'Is there any good reason for you to remain in Mad River?'

Tim sighed. 'I guess not, unless I decide to tangle with Trent and show up his game.'

Old Sam Smith snorted. 'A lot of thanks you'd get for that. And a lot of chance you'd have of doin' it, anyway. Trent is set up here too strong!'

Preacher Abel Gray looked forlorn. 'What our friend says is all too true. Trent has the banker and the judge strongly behind him. They make a hard trio to defeat.'

Sabrina touched Tim's arm. 'I agree with Dad and Mr. Smith. The sensible thing for you to do is to leave Mad River at once. Eventually Trent will go too far and attract attention from the state and federal authorities. And they'll be strong enough to deal with him.'

'And those renegade Injuns as well,' Sam Smith said. 'The gal is plumb right.'

Tim said, 'There is one chore to look after before I go. I aim to call on Sheriff Slade and let her know I'm mighty sad about what happened to Deputy Pete Holm.'

Sabrina frowned. 'There's no need of that. One of us could deliver your message to her.'

113

'No,' Tim said. 'It's something I have to do personal.'

'I think you're being ridiculously sentimental,' Sabrina reprimanded him. And she turned and stood with her back to him.

Tim didn't try to reason with her. He nodded to the two men and went back out into the street. He untied the mare and, swinging into the saddle, nudged her gently in the direction of the jailhouse.

When he got there he was glad to see Susan Slade's horse tied to the hitching post. He'd been worried that he might miss her. He dismounted and went inside the small office. It was empty and silent. As he stood there waiting for Susan Slade, his eyes wandered to the desk, and he saw Pete's worn deputy's star sitting on it. He picked up the star and studied it with sad eyes.

'You keeping score for Trent?' The question was put to him in a tone of contempt, and he glanced up to see that Sheriff Susan Slade had come into the office.

Hastily he put the star back on the desk. 'I'm sorry,' he said. 'I came here to tell you I'm sorry.'

The attractive girl's eyes were scornful. 'Pete was worth a dozen like you.'

'I agree.'

She said, 'Well, errand boy, why did Trent send you here?'

'I'm not doing errands for Trent any

longer.'

She appeared unimpressed. 'Too bad you decided so late, that you had to wait until they shot poor old Pete down!'

'I quit last night before that happened!'

Susan's eyes were bright with anger. 'Trent gave you a good line to fool me with, didn't he? You expect me to believe that?'

'It's the truth.'

'You took Pete in as well,' she said. 'I remember the poor old man saying you were too decent to be lined up on the wrong side of the law. He always had the idea you'd get a stomach full of Trent and turn straight. He sure had you tagged wrong!'

Tim took a step toward her and said urgently, 'You've got to believe me. I feel as bad as you do about Pete.'

'As bad as I do?' she demanded. 'He was like my father!' The girl sheriff's lip quivered, and she began to sob.

The most natural thing to do was to take her in his arms. As he held her close to comfort her, he said, 'Pete was right in at least one thing. I'm fed up with Trent. And I'm finished with him and his crowd.'

Susan looked up at him with tear-filled eyes. 'You're on the level about that?'

'Depend on it,' he said very seriously.

She shook her head in despair. 'What am I going to do? I had so many plans. How can I keep on as sheriff without Pete to help me?'

115

He said, 'You'd be better out of it.'

'But I wanted to stay in office long enough to even things with Trent and the others who killed my father. Now they've murdered Pete as well.'

'They claim it was another Indian raid,' he said.

Defiantly she looked up at him. 'You know as well as I do that the Indians aren't really to blame.'

'I know,' he said worriedly. And giving way to an uncontrollable impulse, he kissed her. Almost at once he let her go. He was prepared for anger on her part. Strangely, she didn't show any.

Staring at him with wondering eyes, she said in a low voice, 'You do feel sorry for me, don't you? You are truly my friend?'

He nodded gravely. 'The kiss was meant as no offense to your office.' He reached out, took one of her hands in his and held it.

She smiled sadly. 'It is awkward, isn't it?'

'You bet. My reputation as a gunman will suffer some if the word gets around I have a habit of kissing sheriffs.'

There was a hint of a twinkle in her lovely gray eyes. 'Depend on me to keep your secret. You say you've broken with Trent. Why are you still in town? You know it can be very dangerous for you.'

'I wanted to say goodbye to some of my friends,' he told her, 'especially you.'

'I see,' she said quietly. 'Where are you going?'

'I don't know.'

'Haven't you any plans at all?'

'No. I haven't bothered making plans for a long spell.'

'Since that half-breed murdered your wife?'

There was a tense silence between them for a moment. He resented her question, and yet, under the circumstances, he couldn't be angry with her. So he just said, 'Maybe.'

'So you're going on to another town and selling your gun to the highest bidder again?'

'Likely.'

'Pete didn't believe you would.'

'Pete didn't know me too well,' he said evenly, wishing she'd get off the subject and let him go.

'I wonder,' she said, studying him with a new expression in her eyes. 'Maybe he understood you better than you think.'

He knew it was time to leave. 'Goodbye, Susan,' he said. 'Good luck.' And he turned to go.

'Tim!'

'Yes?' He looked back over his shoulder.

She was tense as she stared at him. 'You meant that, about going on your aimless way, selling your gun?'

'I suppose so. What else is there?'

Susan took a step toward him and held out her hand. 'But you don't need to leave town.

You can make a deal with me.' And she opened her hand to reveal the deputy's star in its palm.

Tim swallowed hard. 'You're being mighty unrealistic.'

Her eyes met his. 'If you are my friend, as you've claimed to be, you won't leave me in this fix. Pete wouldn't leave me as long as there was a breath of life in him.'

Tim said, 'If I put on that star, it would start a riot in town. Trent would have his men shoot me down pronto.'

She shook her head. 'He wouldn't dare try anything like that openly. You'll be safer with this badge than without it. And I want you to wear it.'

Tim still hesitated.

'The town would never accept me,' he warned her. 'Trent is the mayor, and he'd refuse to let me take office.'

'The sheriff has full authority to pick his deputies,' she told him. 'It's in the town laws. Trent didn't want poor old Pete as deputy, but I wouldn't have anyone else. Take the star.' She urged it on him.

Reluctantly he took the worn star from her hand.

'Pin it on,' she said.

He eyed her with a wry expression on his bronzed face, then pinned it on his shirt front. 'Where does that leave us?'

'You're now a peace officer of Mad River

County,' she told him in an official tone. 'You'll begin your duties as of this moment.'

Glancing at the girl, he asked, 'Now what?'

'You'll police the saloons and the town as Pete did,' she told him. 'And all the while we'll keep working until we get enough evidence on Trent to bring in the federal authorities and settle him for good.'

'It'll be hard to tie him in with Indian raiders.'

Susan frowned. 'You know that's a camouflage.'

'Only partly,' he assured her. 'There are Indians in the gang. I quit because I found out he was selling liquor to Wolf and his cronies.'

'That half-breed,' she said scornfully. 'He and the others who hang around with him are drunkards whom Trent uses to spread this Indian raider lie.'

'Maybe,' he said reluctantly.

Susan smiled at him. 'I'd love to see the faces of some of that gang when you walk into the Lucky Palomino tonight wearing that star.'

Tim felt plenty nervous. And when darkness finally came and it was the hour for him to make the rounds of the various saloons, he began to feel a little shaky.

Beads of perspiration showed at his temples as he touched a hand to one of the swinging doors of the Lucky Palomino. The next moment he was inside. Not many noticed him at first. He saw Flash Moran was busy at the poker table as usual. And he was about to go over to the bar when he saw Jim Trent coming across the room toward him.

Tim stood his ground and waited for Trent. Trent glared at him. 'What kind of a joke is this?'

'No joke. I'm the new deputy.'

'Who told Susan Slade she could appoint you?' the mayor demanded.

'The town laws give her the right,' Tim said calmly.

'In that case we'll change the town laws fast,' was Trent's angry retort.

Tim refused to appear upset, even though he was on edge. He said, 'In the meantime I'll act as deputy.'

'You're a two-bit gun punk trying to act important,' Trent raged. 'I don't want you in my place!'

'And I'm pretty tired of it,' Tim said pleasantly. 'But it happens to be my duty to see there's order kept in here.'

Trent moved in close and in a low voice warned, 'When I said to leave town last night, I wasn't playing around with words. You get goin', or they'll be measurin' you for a right nice sleepin' box.'

Tim eyed the mayor defiantly. 'If that's a threat, I better make note of it,' he said, 'just in case something happens to me.'

'Something will happen to you,' Trent warned. 'Like a hole in your head, maybe!'

Tim didn't let this bother him as he moved on to make the rounds of the other saloons.

That first night ended in triumph. And the following day Tim was congratulated by both Preacher Abel Gray and Sabrina. The blonde girl was thrilled by Tim's decision to wear the deputy's star and told him so.

'I think it's wonderful,' she said. 'I'm glad you decided to do it, even if it is to help another girl.'

Tim smiled thinly. 'I think of it as being the sheriff.'

Sabrina sighed. 'I'd say you've gotten the office and the girl mixed up,' was her verdict.

Tim slipped into the role of deputy with no trouble at all. He and Susan spent a lot of time eagerly discussing how they might make Mad River a safer place to live in. And one afternoon the rancher, Lionel Mason, came to the office and joined in their discussion. It was natural that Tim should question him about the raid on his ranch.

'The night of the raid, did you get a close look at the riders?' he wanted to know.

The gaunt-faced rancher looked troubled. 'It all happened so quickly I had only a fleeting impression,' he admitted. 'But I did plainly see several Indians.'

Tim said, 'Both Susan and I think there are perhaps four or five Indians to fifteen or

121

twenty white outlaws in these raiding parties. That's following the theory that Trent is organizing them.'

'You could be right,' Mason admitted. 'We know the Indians have been getting liquor at the Lucky Palomino. They were crazy wild the night of the raid.'

Susan studied him with troubled eyes. 'Are you saying you think the raiders are actually renegade red men?'

'I can't make up my mind,' the rancher worried. 'I'm very suspicious of Trent, but I did see Indians leading that raiding party.'

After the rancher had gone, Tim and Susan returned to considering the perplexing question. She said, 'Where does this leave us?'

'Just about where we were,' he admitted. 'I know that Trent has some kind of scheme cooked up with Neilson and the judge to get all the land he can before the railway comes through. But I can't be any more certain than Mason whether he's got Indians doing his dirty work or white men masquerading as Indians.'

'We may find out after the next raid,' she said somberly. 'There are bound to be more.'

The town quieted down for a while. Tim came to be accepted as the new deputy. He noticed that Trent and his partners avoided him; other than that everything seemed normal. And then all of a sudden there was

122

more action than he knew how to cope with.

It began one warm, sunny morning when a cowpoke he'd never seen before came riding up in front of the jail and called for the sheriff. Tim went out to see what was up, and the fellow on horseback leaned over to him, wild-eyed.

'Sheriff is wanted at Trent's hardware store,' the rider said.

'What's wrong?' Tim asked.

'I don't know exactly,' the cowboy said. 'Bad trouble, I guess. Banker Neilson is there, and he sent me for the sheriff.'

'She's gone out to one of the ranches,' Tim said. 'But I'll come. Tell Neilson I'll be right there.'

The cowboy rode off, and a few minutes later Tim followed him.

CHAPTER TEN

The band of curious onlookers on the street gave Tim resentful glances as he dismounted and edged his way through the crowd to the door of the hardware store. The pale clerk with the heavy glasses was standing on guard there, and he looked as if he'd had a bad shock. Recognizing Tim, he stepped back and let him into the shadowy store.

Closing the door after them and bolting it,

123

he gave Tim a glance of welcome. 'Sure glad to see you, Deputy,' he said.

'What's wrong?'

The young man looked wary. He licked his pale lips. 'Better find out from Neilson,' he said in a low voice.

Tim frowned at him, then moved down the murky corridor between the counters to the rear of the large store. Near the end of the corridor he discovered the three-hundred-pound Neilson sitting in a chair. He had removed his hat and was wiping perspiration from his bald head. Seeing Tim, he gave a cry of annoyance.

'What are you doing here?' the fat man demanded in his squeaky voice.

Tim halted in front of him. 'You sent for the sheriff.'

'I did. Why are you here in her place?' Neilson was indignant.

'She rode out of town early this morning. I don't expect her back until this afternoon. From the message you sent, I got the idea you needed the law right away.'

'That is true, but I can hardly regard you as a lawman,' Neilson said petulantly.

'I'm duly sworn in,' Tim said. 'But if you don't want my help, I'll move on.' And he turned to leave.

'No! Wait a minute!' Neilson had gotten to his feet with an agility surprising in one of his enormous weight.

Tim turned to him again. 'Well?'

The fat man was breathing heavily, and his face was a nasty purplish color. 'It seems I don't have any choice,' he said brokenly. 'I'll have to turn to you. Something terrible has happened back there.' He indicated Trent's office.

Tim's curiosity was whetted to a peak point. 'What?'

Neilson's face mirrored his horror. The fat man said, 'Go see for yourself!'

Tim gave the banker a questioning look and then pushed by him. Farther down the corridor, he came on a body stretched out on the floor. It was the half-breed, Wolf. Tim bent down to examine the renegade and see if he were still living. He was alive, but in a coma from alcohol, judging by the smell. Tim rose in disgust and continued on to the steps leading to Trent's office.

The first thing he noticed was that the lamp was still burning in the office, though it was morning. And then he saw Trent sitting slumped in his swivel chair before his desk. His head was bent forward on his chest, and he gave no hint of being aware of Tim's entrance. It was only when Tim took a second, closer look that the full horror of the scene hit him.

Trent had been scalped! The knife used in the scalping was on the floor near the swivel chair, and so was Trent's scalp.

125

With a feeling of revulsion, Tim turned away and went back down to the main body of the store.

He stepped over the snoring, motionless Wolf again and went on until he came face to face with the shaken Neilson.

'I never thought a thing like this could happen,' he said in a hoarse whisper.

'Appears that Trent must have riled Wolf about something. Then the half-breed got liquored up and came back here and finished him off in Indian style.'

Neilson stared at him, his heavy jowls quivering. 'Wolf is still dead drunk. How could he have managed it?'

'He probably loaded himself with booze after he killed Trent,' was Tim's opinion. 'If we look, I've an idea we'll find the half-breed raided the liquor supplies.'

'Yes,' the fat man agreed. And then anger replaced his terror, and he said, 'Wolf's neck has to be stretched for this. It'll be a lesson for the other Sioux around here.'

'He'll answer to the law,' Tim assured him. 'But I don't see how hanging one half-breed is going to settle the trouble with the Indians you people started.'

The fat man gasped. 'What are you trying to say?'

'That I know Trent and you and the judge set up most of those so-called Indian raids, and Wolf was one of your henchmen. Maybe

126

he'll decide to talk and tell us some of the things we need as proof.'

Neilson stared at him. 'Would you listen to a thief and a killer; take his word against the word of a man like me or the judge?'

Tim eyed him sternly. 'I would, though I can't speak for anyone else.'

'Don't you go too far, Parker! I warn you!' The fat man pointed a stubby finger at him. 'I demand Wolf be jailed at once and the sheriff informed of what has happened.'

'Glad to oblige,' Tim said. 'As a deputy, I'm paid to look after the welfare of all the citizens. Even dubious characters like Trent and you have to be protected. So Wolf goes to jail.'

The fat man was trembling with anger. 'The sheriff will hear about the way you behaved here. I promise you that. And I also promise you that you won't be wearing that deputy's badge long!'

Tim gave him a slow smile. 'I reckon you see yourself as the power in town now that Trent is out of the way. Too bad you don't take it as a warning of what could happen to you.'

'Don't you dare threaten me!' Neilson squealed in rage.

Tim paid no further attention to him. He went back to the still snoring half-breed and, lifting him from the floor, slung him over his shoulder like a sack. Then he marched out of

127

the store and rode back with his prisoner to the jail.

He sent word out to Susan, and she came back to town early. By the time she arrived, Wolf was beginning to come around. The groaning from his cell was piteous and could be heard all through the jailhouse. Tim had never seen Susan so shaken by anything. She came back after seeing the half-breed with a face that was white and distressed. Standing with Tim in the tiny office, she asked, 'What do you make of it?'

'Trent deserved what happened to him,' Tim suggested. 'Maybe Neilson and the judge will learn from it and go slow with their power play from now on.'

She nodded. 'I suppose it's as simple as that.'

There was a doubt in her voice that startled him. 'You don't seem too convinced,' he said. 'There isn't any big mystery about what happened as far as I'm concerned.'

'That's one of the reasons I wonder,' she said, her gray eyes fixing on him earnestly. 'The evidence is black against the half-breed. And yet I don't think Wolf is the type to kill in that fashion.'

'He's half Indian,' Tim reminded her. 'And he was crazy with drink.'

'You're ready to believe anything bad about Indians, aren't you?'

'What's that got to do with it?'

She sighed. 'Nothing, I guess. But it seems to me most people around here feel the same way. There won't be any questions asked. Wolf will be found guilty, and the judge will sentence him to hang.'

'Admitting that Trent deserved what he got, the penalty for murder is hanging. I can see no reason why Wolf shouldn't pay for his crime.'

'Yes,' she said quietly, 'if it is his crime.'

But except for Susan, few people in town showed any doubts concerning Wolf's guilt. Tim felt the only two exceptions, besides the sheriff, were preacher Abel Gray and his daughter, Sabrina. The two came to the jailhouse to visit the prisoner. And while her father lingered in the cell with the half-breed, Sabrina came out to the office to give Tim her views.

'Dad doesn't think Wolf killed the mayor,' she said. 'He often came to our mission. And he showed a desire to stop his drinking. He was one of the friendliest of the Indians.'

'Sorry,' Tim said. 'I know more about the case than your father. And I have no doubt that Wolf is the murderer. I was there and found the body and Wolf drunk not thirty feet away.'

'It's still circumstantial evidence,' she insisted. 'No one saw the crime committed.'

Tim smiled wearily. 'I doubt if the court needs to produce a witness to the killing. The

129

facts speak for themselves.'

The blonde girl looked worried. 'You're so coldly sure about this. It isn't typical of you. Is it because Wolf is a half-breed? Are you letting your prejudice sway you?'

He felt his cheeks burn. 'I've never pretended I liked Indians,' he said. 'But I do try to be fair.'

'I hope so, Tim,' the pretty blonde said, studying him. 'I've had such high hopes for you since you took this job. I wouldn't want anything to spoil it.'

'Nothing will.'

'You haven't come around to the mission lately,' she reminded him. 'We've missed you.'

'I've been busy,' he said awkwardly.

Preacher Abel Gray came to join his daughter, and the two left together.

As time passed, the tension in the jailhouse reflected the growing tension in the town. Only two days remained until Wolf's trial, and everyone knew he was going to be judged guilty and there would be a stringing up immediately thereafter. Tim had never felt so cut off from the lovely girl sheriff. They both went soberly about their work, and neither said much.

When Preacher Abel Gray and Sabrina made their visits to the jail, Tim arranged it so that it was Susan who was there to greet them. Her views on the prisoner's guilt coincided with that of the Grays. And he didn't want to discuss the case with any of them.

If things had looked bad for Wolf, they became a lot worse the day before his trial. In the morning, a rider came into Mad River with the news that the renegade Indians had staged another raid on the Mason ranch the previous night. This time Deputy Pete Holm and his men weren't there to defend the homestead, and the ranch house had been burned to the ground and Mason killed. Neighbors had come to the rescue of his wife and children, but most of the Mason stock had been taken. There was no question but that the ranch was finished as a going concern.

The news had a stunning impact on Mad River. Tempers rose to a new high. The resentment against the Sioux had never been greater. It made the worst possible climate for Wolf's trial. Tim expected Susan to take the news badly, and she did.

She said, 'This was deliberate! Neilson and the judge timed this raid to make sure their hand-picked jury convicts Wolf!'

'I don't agree,' Tim protested. 'They probably staged it last night because it suited them.'

'The whole thing is a mockery of justice,' Susan stormed. 'I know who is behind the raids, and I can't say. You can head the posse that goes out there to investigate, I want no part of it!'

And she stuck to her resolution. Tim gathered up a half-dozen riders and swore them in as a posse. Then he took them out to the Mason ranch. It was a sad sight, with the burned logs of the ranch house still smoldering a little. As usual, the raiders had vanished without a trace.

Tim picked up all the information he could, but it wasn't much. Those who had seen the raiding party and lived to tell about it were badly confused in their accounts. They all agreed that Indians had done the damage, but few could give any descriptions of them. Tim felt almost as sick at heart as he knew Susan must be. The whole business had a familiar ring to it. He kept thinking back to the murder of his own wife and his frustration when he had found out the law wouldn't do anything to avenge her murder; that the only justice offered was crooked justice!

Now he felt he might be representing that same kind of justice. However badly he wanted to make someone pay for Mason's killing, he knew he could only go so far; that the leaders behind the evil raids were among the elite in the small cow town. And unless he could dig up some real proof of the connection between them and the raids, he would get nowhere.

That night he rode back to town with the

posse, having accomplished nothing. He'd spent a hard day in the hills and the adjoining desert country under a burning sun. He'd never felt more thoroughly weary in his life.

When he entered the office of the jail, Susan was sitting at her desk. The lamp hanging from the ceiling of the tiny room was smoking slightly and giving off more fumes than light. At first Susan didn't turn to greet him. He walked across the room to stand by the desk before she glanced up.

She said, 'You look done in.'

'I am,' he admitted.

'Well?'

'Nothing,' he said, anger coming into his voice. 'Like all the other raids. Nothing left and no chance of tracing the raiders.'

'I expected that,' she said quietly.

He frowned and stared at her, aware for the first time that she was in a strangely resigned mood. He said, 'You seem to be taking all this pretty coolly.'

'I suppose I am,' she agreed.

'You were in a state when I left,' he reminded her. 'Now you're just as peaceful as a cream-fed kitten. Are you forgetting that Wolf stands trial tomorrow?'

'No,' she said, rising.

'Well?'

'I guess you'd better be the first to hear,' she said. 'Wolf isn't going to stand trial.'

There was a tense moment of silence. He

133

stared at her. 'Why not?'

'He escaped while you were away. I went in to give him his meal tonight, and he overpowered me and got free.'

Tim couldn't believe it. 'Didn't you sound an alarm, let the town know he'd broken jail?'

'It happened only a little while ago,' she said. 'He took my horse. I decided to wait until you got back.'

Her calmness was unnatural. The suspicion that had been fast growing in his mind could no longer be contained. With an accusing look, he asked, 'You set him free, didn't you?'

CHAPTER ELEVEN

The girl sheriff didn't flick an eyelid. 'Why do you say that?' she asked.

'I'm certain that you did.'

'In that case, there's no use trying to change your mind,' she said in a calm voice.

Tim quickly considered what this would mean if the word got out. If the citizens of Mad River ever guessed what she'd done, the chances were they'd want to string her up or at least tar and feather her and run her out of town on a rail. He had to go along with her story and try to protect her.

He said, 'This wasn't smart or even wise,

134

Susan.'

'I couldn't let them murder him. That's what they've been looking forward to doing.'

Tim eyed her with despair. 'We'll have to change your story; say it happened later, that I came back here and found you locked in the cell. Otherwise they're going to want to know why you didn't give out a warning that he'd escaped.'

'You needn't cover for me,' she said primly.

'I needn't but I will,' he said with a groan. 'This is what comes of making a female a sheriff!'

'I had to do it, Tim!' For the first time there was urgency in her voice and in her expression.

He patted her arm. 'I know,' he said.

'You were as bad as the others. Because he's an Indian, you didn't care what happened to him.'

'All right,' he said wearily. 'We've been over that ground before. Let's get our story straight and spread the good news about Wolf getting away.'

Tim's version of things was far from perfect, but he did manage to make the town believe it. The escape of the half-breed caused a sensation. It also caused a lot of uneasiness in certain quarters.

The most unexpected development in this respect was the arrival of a nervous Flash

Moran at the jail to demand special protection for himself and the Lucky Palomino saloon. The diamond in the gambler's front tooth sparkled as he stammered his way through his request. His coarse, florid face was wet with sweat as he stood in the center of the small office.

With a scowl at Tim, who was standing in the corner taking it all in, he turned to the girl sheriff again and said, 'Wolf has a special grudge against me and the saloon. As long as he's on the loose, I'm in danger.'

From her desk, Susan asked calmly, 'What reason has he to hate you so much, Moran?'

Moran looked guilty. 'He's a crazy half-breed! Isn't that reason enough! They get fool hatreds against people!'

'I've not found that,' Susan said.

The gambler glared at her. 'I know you and your deputy friend have it in for me,' he said. 'But I deserve protection the same as anyone else!'

'And you'll get it the same as anyone else,' she told him.

Flash Moran hesitated a moment, and then, with an angry look for both of them, he turned and stomped out of the office. There was a momentary silence in the warm room, broken only by the buzzing of a fly against the windowpane.

Susan offered him a bleak smile. 'Your old friend seems to be worried.'

136

'So I notice,' he said, staring at the doorway through which Moran had just left. 'And I always thought he and Wolf were on good terms.'

'So did I,' she agreed. 'Could it be there's someone else he's afraid of, and that he doesn't want to say?'

'It's possible.'

'I think we should keep a close eye on Moran and notice whom he sees,' was Susan's suggestion.

Several days passed, during which there was no criminal activity in Mad River other than a shooting brawl in which one of the combatants was winged, and the usual daily routine of drunk and disorderly arrests in the saloons. It was Susan's custom to get drunks out of the jail as soon as they had sobered in the morning. Whenever possible, she collected a fine. But there were some derelict repeaters to whom money was a complete stranger. Tim generally approved of her system. It kept the town from having to pay food bills for a lot of no-goods.

During the court trial of the two who'd been engaged in a gun fight in front of the Lucky Palomino, the emaciated Judge Gordon Parsons presided. When sentence had been passed and a fine collected, the justice dismissed the court but kept both Sheriff Susan Slade and Tim there to give them a lecture.

'I will not put up with slackness in the running of the sheriff's office,' the old man warned them in his querulous voice. 'And unless Wolf is apprehended, I warn you there will be a change made in personnel.'

Susan listened in grave silence. 'We'll do what we can, Judge,' she promised.

The old man squinted at her suspiciously. 'I wonder if that will be enough.'

Later, when they were out in the street, Tim told her, 'I'm sure he's onto us. He knows Wolf was deliberately set free.'

Susan shrugged. 'He knows it in the same way we know who's responsible for the raids. He can't prove anything.'

'The day may come,' Tim warned.

But he'd not dreamed then what the next development would be, or that when they saw the judge again he'd be a rigid corpse. The old man had not been seen around the town for several days when banker Neil Neilson came to the sheriff's office and demanded that they break into the judge's house.

'Parsons has missed several meetings with me,' the fat man said in his squeaky voice. 'Something has to be wrong. He lives alone, and his place has been locked tight whenever I've sent a messenger to him. That never happened before.'

'We'll look into it,' Susan promised.

The fat man's perspiring pink face showed fear. 'You better.'

Tim rode along with her. He knew the judge had the reputation of being a miser, that he was a bachelor who lived frugally without even a cook. In fact, he'd frequently seen him having meals in the town's cheapest restaurant. And there was a standing joke that he always ordered the least expensive dish on the menu. It was known as Judge Parsons' special.

When they reached the isolated white frame house, they found all the entrances to it locked. But Tim discovered a door to the cellar, and there were steps from it leading up into the main house. He gave Susan the choice of waiting outside or going with him.

'I'll go with you,' she said.

Tim had a hunch the old man had died, maybe in his sleep. He kept well ahead as they moved up into the main living quarters. He wanted to spare Susan any unpleasantness or shock. It was just as well he'd operated on that theory. They found the judge on the floor of his study. And he'd been scalped, just as Trent had been.

Tim hastily shoved Susan back so she had only a glimpse of the bloody mutilated figure stretched out in the small dark room. The circumstances were almost identical with those of Trent's murder. The judge had been stabbed for good measure, and his scalp was left on the floor beside him.

Susan leaned against the wall in the

hallway, looking as if she might be going to faint. Tim offered her his arm for support. But he couldn't resist saying, 'You were determined to let Wolf go free.'

She turned to him vaguely. 'I don't believe Wolf did it.'

'Who else then?'

'I don't know,' she confessed.

Tim glanced toward the study door, a grim expression on his young face. 'I don't figure banker Neilson is going to be overjoyed about this. It's getting pretty close to home.'

He was correct. Mad River was a town without proper law enforcement, according to the irate and terrified banker Neilson. The fat man had hired a couple of tough characters to guard him day and night. It was quite a sight to see him driving along the main street in his buggy with the two gunmen riding along beside him.

Tim was of the opinion it would only be a matter of a week or so before the state authorities came to investigate the happenings of Mad River and turned both him and Susan out of office. There was every likelihood that the banker had sent a message to the capital about the Indian uprising in the area.

Susan disagreed. She pointed out that Neil Neilson wouldn't dare appeal to the state, since it could mean his part in the raids would be revealed. 'He won't take a chance,' she reported to Tim with satisfaction.

'At least we know Wolf is the killer and can be on the lookout for him,' Tim said.

'The killer could be anyone. I say it's probably not an Indian. The scalping business is a trick to throw us off the track.'

'I don't think anyone but an Indian would go to that trouble,' Tim argued. 'It's not a white man's way of killing!'

She smiled coldly. 'So we're back to your Indian prejudices again.'

Tim gave her a solemn look. 'I think it's way past time I got out of this town,' he said. And he walked out of the jailhouse and left her.

One night when Tim was patrolling the town, he approached the store where the Reverend Abel Gray had established his mission. He waited as he saw the door open and a small band of the faithful come out. Standing in the shadows, he counted a few children, two Indian women, several of the village women in their bonnets and a couple of the broken-down drunks who regularly stationed themselves in front of the various saloons to beg drinks.

When the group scattered, Tim moved on. But just as he came abreast of the door, Sabrina Gray appeared in the doorway. She smiled and said, 'Where have you been keeping yourself?'

'Busy,' he told her. 'You know we've had another murder.'

'Yes,' she said, her face somber. 'I've had problems as well. Father is ill, and I've had to take on the mission duties alone.'

'I just saw your flock,' he said with a grim smile.

She sighed. 'I know. We get only a few children and the really desperate.'

'I hope your father isn't seriously ill,' he said.

The blonde girl appeared worried. 'It's hard to say. The doctor doesn't seem to be able to tell what is wrong. Father has lost a lot of weight, and he has a good deal of pain. The doctor gives him medicine, but he doesn't seem to get any better.'

'I'm sorry,' Tim said sincerely.

Sabrina said, 'Won't you come in and visit with him for a moment? He enjoys seeing his friends.'

Tim had his rounds to make and was anxious to get on his way. But he didn't want to hurt the feelings of the girl or her father. So he said, 'If it won't disturb him, I'd like to stop by for a few minutes.'

The girl looked pleased. 'He's in his bedroom,' she said, and led Tim through the mission to the door leading to the rear of the house.

The preacher's bedroom was tiny, and a candle flickered on the worn dresser, which was the single item of furniture in it besides the bed. The quiet man lay back on his pillow

142

with his eyes closed. Tim was shocked by his changed appearance. In a very short time he'd lost a great deal of weight.

Sabrina leaned over the bed and in a gentle voice said, 'Father, it's Tim Parker. He's stopped by to speak to you.'

The preacher's eyes opened, and he looked up at Tim with a weary smile. 'How nice of you, Tim.'

'Sorry to find you ill, sir,' Tim said respectfully.

'It is a nuisance,' the sick man agreed. He gave Sabrina a fond smile. 'However, my daughter is seeing that our work is not interrupted. Don't you think that's wonderful?'

'I do,' Tim agreed.

'I worried that I might have to leave Mad River with our work not finished,' the preacher said. 'But Sabrina has taken over and given me new heart. Soon I'll be well enough to help her.'

'I'm sure of that,' Tim said.

He stayed a few minutes more before leaving. The sick man seemed to drift off into sleep again, and Tim guessed the doctor had drugged him heavily against his pain. He quietly made his way to the door and out.

Sabrina saw him to the wooden sidewalk. Her pretty young face showed concern as she asked, 'Do you think he looks very ill?'

Tim hedged, anxious not to worry her

needlessly. 'He has failed, but he could soon put weight on again when he begins to recover.'

'I hope so,' she said, but her voice indicated that she didn't believe it.

'If he should get any worse or if you need help, you can reach me at the jail,' Tim reminded her. 'I want to know how he is.'

'I'll remember,' she said. 'Thanks.' And she went back into the mission and closed the door.

Tim felt sorry for the lovely girl. Upset by the discovery of the preacher's illness, he crossed the street and headed for the Lucky Palomino.

Of late he had made it one of his regular visiting places. Flash Moran had not put up a protest about his intrusions. It was Tim's hunch the gambler was now glad to see him around. Both Moran and the fat banker seemed to be living in mortal fear of the renegade Wolf. Tim wondered what double-cross they had pulled on the half-breed to earn his hatred.

The usual stragglers were grouped around the saloon's swinging doors, and the same honky-tonk piano was being played. Tim entered the noisy, crowded room and, seeing an empty place at the bar, went over and ordered a whiskey. His deputy's star was always pay enough for as much as he wanted to drink in any of the saloons. He'd barely downed the whiskey when a hand touched his left shoulder. He turned around to see Flash Moran standing there.

But it wasn't a belligerent Moran this time. It was a shaken, subdued version of the flamboyant gambler he'd known. Moran's coarse face was abnormally red, as if he'd been drinking too much. And when he spoke, his voice was slurred.

'Always welcome in the place, Parker,' he said.

'Glad to hear it,' Tim said evenly, noting that Moran was drunker than he'd ever seen him.

The eyes with their broken red veins studied him. 'No hard feelings?'

'None,' Tim assured him.

'Good!' the gambler said with drunken solemnity. 'I'm counting on you to get that no-account Wolf. The town is counting on you!'

'I know.'

Moran lifted a hand regally. 'I'll see you get a reward—extra money!'

'Thanks,' Tim said in a dry voice. 'I'll remember that.'

Moran swayed a little and seemed about to go on with his harangue when he glanced in the direction of the entrance and suddenly seemed to change his mind. He weaved off toward the rear of the saloon as if the devil were on his heels.

145

Tim stared after him and then turned to order a second whiskey. He downed the second drink and was ready to leave when a familiar figure edged in at the bar beside him. It was the wizened little Sam Smith. The eccentric old prospector looked the same as ever.

Jutting out his scruffy black beard, the little man said, 'Soon as I saw you, I decided I wanted to treat you to a drink.'

Tim smiled. 'I've already had a couple. And if I recall rightly, drinking with you nearly always leads to a lot of trouble.'

Sam Smith chuckled. 'Don't believe that!' And he ordered for them. Glancing around the saloon, he asked, 'Where's Moran?'

'Too drunk to show himself,' Tim said. 'He just staggered away.'

The grizzled prospector made a face. 'Bad business! When a fella like him starts hitting the booze like that, it means he's lost his nerve. And a gambler without nerve might as well be dead.'

'It's the fear of being dead that has started him drinking,' Tim said.

'Oh?'

He nodded. 'Moran is sure that Wolf is coming after him, that he'll be scalped, like Trent and the judge.'

The old man smiled slyly. 'According to the stories I hear, that Injun stripped the top of their heads off just as neat as you like!'

Leaning close to Tim, he went on with relish, 'You know how it's done, don't you? They slit right around above the eyes to the back of the head nice and neat and even. Right through the hair and skin and muscle the knife goes, and then the Injun flips up the skin and takes it between his teeth and yanks the whole top off the head!' He finished with a loud cackle of laughter.

Tim was sickened by the description. He said, 'I saw both those men, and what you told me just now brought it all back. It was a mighty ugly sight.'

'Redskins think a scalp gives them extra strength and power. I seen more than one scalping in my time.'

'I guess Moran has a right to be scared,' Tim said.

'And fatty Neilson! They tell me he has special guards to watch him.' The little man chuckled. 'That ain't goin' to do him any good if that Injun decides to settle with him.'

Tim frowned. 'What do you think started Wolf on this scalping spree?'

'Does an Injun need a good reason?' the little man wanted to know. 'Those Sioux of mine are too quiet these days. It wouldn't surprise me if they took a sudden notion to turn on me and finish me off fast-like.'

'Why do you keep them on at the castle, then?'

'Mainly because I can't get anyone else to

stay there with me,' the old prospector said with a resigned look on his wrinkled face. 'And anyway, I'm an old man, and it don't matter too much what happens to me.'

Tim smiled. 'Not everyone is so fatalistic.'

'That's a right fancy word,' the old man marveled. 'I like you, Tim. I always did, even when you was totin' a gun for Trent.'

'That didn't last long.'

'You like being deputy better?'

Tim shook his head. 'It's just a matter of selling my gun on the right side of the law. I'd like to be able to put away my .44 for all time.'

The wizened veteran with the black beard eyed him sharply. 'You're living in the wrong country for that, son.'

'There were years when I never used a gun,' Tim told him, 'back when I had my own ranch.'

Sam Smith's smile was knowing. 'That was before the Injuns came and raided your peaceful valley and finished off your wife. You told me about it. And I don't blame you for feeling as you do about redskins.'

'I'd rather not talk about it,' Tim said.

'Sorry,' the prospector apologized. 'Thing is, I can't understand how an Injun hater like yourself would let Wolf get out of jail so easy.'

'I had nothing to do with it. It happened when I was out.'

148

'Did it?' Sam Smith showed unusual interest. 'I think we both ought to have a whiskey on that. It's a wonder I didn't hit on it before.'

Tim glanced at the old man. 'Hit on what?'

'The reason that redskin got away so neat,' the old man said with a wink. And he ordered the drinks.

Tim was uneasy. He began to think the old prospector had guessed that Susan had deliberately freed Wolf. And if Sam Smith had hit on the truth, others might soon do the same. If that happened, both he and Susan would be in hot water.

He took his whiskey and downed it. Then he looked at the old man and said, 'What are you talking about?'

The wizened face had a crafty expression. 'I know you're pretty sweet on Susan, so I ain't goin' to say any more right now. I tell you what. When you get back to the sheriff's office, you let her know what I said: that Sam Smith says he knows why she didn't keep that half-breed behind bars.'

'She won't understand,' Tim told him.

'I think she will,' the prospector said with a wink. And he nudged Tim in the ribs with a skinny elbow.

'You try, anyway.'

Tim left the little man still standing at the bar and went out of the Lucky Palomino with his head in a whirl. And it wasn't the whiskey

that was bothering him. Sam Smith had
started him worrying about Susan. He was
sure the old man knew something about her
that Tim didn't. And whatever it was, it
wouldn't be good news at this time.

He made the rest of his rounds as quickly
as he could, then rode the mare back to the
jail. Susan was in the sheriff's office when he
went inside, and she gave him a surprised
look.

'What's troubling you?' she asked.

'Do I show it that much?' he wanted to
know as he seated himself on the edge of her
desk and stared down at her.

'You look haunted,' she said.

He frowned. 'I met old Sam Smith in town.
And he said something that started me
worrying—something about you.'

The girl wearing the sheriff's star showed
no betraying expression. 'What did he say?'

'He said he knew why you didn't keep
Wolf behind bars,' Tim told her. 'And he
said it as if it had a secret meaning.'

Her smile was bitter. 'I guess maybe it
has.'

'He said you'd explain.'

Susan had risen from her chair. She said, 'I
should have told you before. I didn't because
I didn't think you'd like it.'

'What?' he asked sharply.

'I happen to be part Indian,' she said
simply. 'I'm one quarter Sioux.'

150

CHAPTER TWELVE

Tim stood there, stunned by her words. Then, after a moment, he demanded, 'Why didn't you tell me before?'

Her eyes reproached him. 'I knew how you felt about Indians; all Indians. I wanted you to like me.'

'It has nothing to do with my liking you,' he said almost angrily. 'I should have known. How many people in Mad River besides old Sam know about this?'

'I don't think there's anyone,' she said. 'Sam was a friend of my father's. At least my father took pity on the old man. One night when they were here talking, Dad let it drop that his mother had been a full-blooded Sioux.'

'Old Sam sure didn't forget it,' Tim said in a troubled voice. 'He suggested that was the reason you were so sympathetic to Wolf.'

'He might be right. I do feel close to the Indians. I think the settlers have abused them.'

Tim's handsome face was shadowed with concern. 'There's no point in debating that now. We can only hope Sam Smith doesn't mention this to anyone else. If talk got around town that you were part Indian, there's no telling what they'd conclude.'

Her smile was wry. 'That perhaps I'd deliberately let Wolf go?'

'Probably.'

'We'll have to wait and see.'

'Meanwhile, that crazy half-breed is at large and has the town in a sweat. Flash Moran came up to me tonight dead drunk. He's so frightened of Wolf he's drinking himself to death.'

'That would be a suitable ending for a character like him,' Susan said.

'I'm not worried about Moran,' Tim admitted. 'But I sure am uneasy about us.'

'Sam won't talk. He only told you because he was drinking too much,' she said.

'I hope you're right,' he said grimly. He remembered the old prospector had still been drinking when he had left the saloon. It was hard to tell to whom he'd be talking or what he'd say before the night was over.

*   *   *

The day Lionel Mason's widow and children took the stage out of Mad River after selling the ranch to the syndicate, Tim was summoned to banker Neil Neilson's office. The grossly fat survivor of the evil trio for whom Tim had first worked was waiting for him.

Neilson waved a dainty hand, indicating Tim should sit down. 'What I have to discuss

152

may take a little time, Deputy.'

Tim sat down. He could feel the banker's greedy little eyes appraising him. He said, 'Is there anything wrong?'

The fat man laughed a mirthless, high-pitched laugh. 'That's a foolish question to ask,' he said. 'You know I never go anywhere without guards any more, and you ask me if there's anything wrong!'

'We're trying to smoke out Wolf,' Tim said.

The fat man, looking more like an indignant Humpty Dumpty than ever, showed a nasty expression. 'I'd like to believe that.'

'We are.'

Neilson leaned forward over the desk and said, 'Frankly, I'm sick of beating about the bush. Let's talk straight. I'm not satisfied with the present sheriff or the kind of job she's doing. I never did want her to have the office. It's made Mad River a laughingstock. And now that she's failed to give us protection from the Indians, I'm all for getting rid of her and making a new appointment.'

'I see,' Tim said.

'You can have the job, Parker,' the fat man said. 'I'm willing to forget the past, because I know you're a good man with a gun, and I want you on my side. All I ask is that you bring Wolf in by the end of the week. That

153

gives you a reasonable length of time. I'm
sure you've got a hunch where the varmint is.
Just waiting for the right deal, eh, Parker?'

Tim tried to hide his distaste for the gross
banker.

'I'll give it some thought,' he promised.

'I knew you'd see it my way,' Neilson said
gleefully. 'I'll be naming the next sheriff in
this town. And if it happens to be you, I can
promise you a rich future.'

'In what way?'

Greed welled up in the fat face. 'The
railroad is coming, Parker. There'll be more
than enough greenbacks for all of us. You
think this country is prosperous now? Wait
until you see it then. And I'll be running the
whole district, with you as my right-hand
man.'

Tim couldn't help but smile at the banker's
vivid picture. He said, 'You make it pretty
tempting.'

'The offer of a lifetime, Parker. Don't pass
it up.'

'What about Susan Slade?' Tim asked.
'Where does she fit in?'

The fat man scowled. 'I haven't decided
about her. But if she's lucky, she'll be
allowed to leave town. I don't want her
around once she's out of that office.'

'I wouldn't like to see anything happen to
her.'

'She doesn't worry about what happens to

other people.' The fat man fairly squealed with annoyance. 'She let that half-breed escape, and I'm at the top of his list.'

Tim asked the question he'd put to the judge before the latter was scalped. He said, 'Why? What has Wolf got against you?'

Neilson grimaced. 'He's got some fool idea we didn't pay him enough for some work he did for us. Truth is, we gave him more than he was worth.'

'Did you pay what you promised?' Tim wanted to know. 'Indians respect people who keep their word.'

The tiny eyes of the banker regarded him with suspicion. 'You suddenly talk like an Injun lover! Somebody convert you?'

Tim flushed. 'No. I'm just stating a fact. If you broke your word to Wolf, you might have expected trouble.'

'It doesn't matter now,' the banker said. 'You and I have a deal. You're going to finish off that half-breed in return for becoming sheriff.'

'I'll see what I can manage,' Tim said, rising. 'Is that all?'

'That's all, Parker,' the fat man said. 'I've tagged you as a smart operator from the night I first met you in Trent's office. Now's your chance to prove it. You don't have to bring Wolf in. Just put a bullet between his eyes, and I'll be satisfied.'

Tim nodded. 'When I find out anything,

I'll let you know,' he said.

He walked out of the bank in a grim mood. Neilson had nerve, thinking he could bribe him into doublecrossing Susan. There was no amount of cash which could make him do that. He'd played along with the fat man to keep him from making the same offer to anyone else. But this was one of Neilson's schemes that was going to backfire.

The remark about him being an Indian lover hadn't gone over well, either. It was true he'd undergone a change in his feelings toward red men in the past week. Experience had shown him that there were evil members of every race, and it was ridiculous to heap blame on any given group of people for the wrongs done by a few. The knowledge that Susan was one fourth Sioux had helped reveal the fallacy of his previous thinking. His hatred against redskins had evaporated, and even Neilson had sensed it.

As he rode down the main street on his piebald mare, he came near the store where the preacher and his daughter had their chapel, and saw a small group of youngsters and a few older folk standing forlornly outside the door.

At once he sensed something was wrong. Reining the mare, he called out to one of the children. The boy came running over, and Tim asked him, 'What's going on at the mission?'

The lad was wide-eyed with sorrow. 'Preacher is dead,' he said.

Tim had guessed it. He said, 'That's too bad.' And he rode on to the jail.

Susan was out, but when she returned Tim told her the news. The dark girl looked sad. 'That's a shame,' she said. 'I must go and call on Sabrina.'

'That would be nice,' Tim agreed.

Susan's eyes questioned him. 'What will she do now? She'll never be able to run that mission alone, not in this wild country.'

He considered. 'She's been doing pretty well with it.'

'But she had her father with her, even though he was ill,' Susan pointed out. 'Now she'll have no one, unless—' She hesitated.

'Unless what?' Tim asked her.

The attractive dark girl said, 'Unless she finds a husband, and quickly. What about you, Tim? I know you like her.'

Tim sighed. 'I like her. She's a fine girl, But I never was in love with her.'

'Are you still deliberately shutting all emotion out of your life?' Susan wanted to know.

'Maybe,' he said. 'I'm not sure.'

'You should be,' was Susan's advice.

They both paid a mourning call on the unfortunate Sabrina. The blonde girl was close to a state of shock. But from what little she managed to say, Tim gathered that the

157

missionary society which had sponsored her father's work would do no more than pay her way back East. They would not consider it practical to support her in the endeavor. And Sabrina seemed ready to leave the frontier country where her father had spent his last days.

The preacher's funeral was surprisingly well attended, and a great deal of sympathy was extended to the grieving Sabrina. As Tim rode back from the cemetery, he realized the end of the week was at hand and he'd not done anything to placate banker Neil Neilson, who was waiting for him to bring word that he'd finished off the half-breed, Wolf.

He worried about this for the rest of the day. And that night, when he was making his rounds of the town, he decided to stop by the bank and see if Neilson was there. He often came back to work at night. There was no light in the front section of the bank, but he could see a reflection through the window of the private office Neilson had at the rear of the building. Tim got down from the mare and tied her to the hitching post. Then he tried the front door of the bank. To his surprise, it opened at his touch. This puzzled him, and at the same time he wondered where the banker's two guards were. He always had them with him when he came back after dark. There was no sign of them now.

Hesitantly he made his way down the dark

length of the bank until he reached the partly opened door to Neilson's private office. Light streamed through it. He stepped up to the door and pushed it open. What he saw came as no surprise. Neilson was sitting behind his desk, staring at him with wide-open, terrified eyes.

But the Humpty Dumpty head had been neatly scalped. Blood dripped down from the mutilated area as the fat man sat there in death, looking remarkably as he had in life. Tim didn't even need to check to know Neilson was dead and that the facts of the crime would match those of the previous two scalpings. Wolf had settled his score with the last of the trio. There would be only Flash Moran left!

Tim put a man on guard at the bank and sent a message to Susan. Then he located the guards. They were stretched out, drugged, in an outbuilding. Later they told him a weird story about finding a rum bottle in one of their saddle bags.

Susan rode up to the bank shortly after Tim sent word he needed her. She didn't go in to see the banker's mutilated body, but stood in the outer area while he filled her in on the details. When he finished, she gave a deep sigh.

She said, 'I guess this settles it. I have to blame Wolf.'

'I warned you from the start,' he said.

The dark girl looked deathly pale. 'I believed his story. He told it so honestly. I had no idea he had a twisted mind.'

'Don't think about it,' Tim cautioned her. 'You acted as you thought best.'

'I took the law into my own hands,' she said unhappily. 'And I had no right to do that. As a result, I'm responsible for the deaths of both the judge and Neilson.'

'Don't look at it that way.'

'There's no other way,' she told him. 'I have no right to wear a lawman's badge. I should resign tonight.'

'Let's not do anything hasty,' he said. 'Since we know it's Wolf we're after, I'll spend my time in tracking him down. I'll start tonight.'

'Where?' she asked. 'We have no idea of his hiding place. You could search the hills for months and not discover it.'

Tim's whole manner had become one of dedicated resolve. He said, 'I'll start at the Lucky Palomino. Flash Moran was the contact man between Trent and the others and Wolf. I'll question him. He wants Wolf brought in. If he knows anything, he's bound to tell me.'

'Tim, do you think so?' There was some hope in her voice.

'I'm sure of it,' he said. And very briefly he took her in his arms and kissed her. Then he went out into the night and, finding his mare, rode on to the Lucky Palomino.

He found Flash Moran in his private office, slumped on the desk, his head resting on his arms. The gambler was drunk, as had been the pattern lately. Tim shook him roughly and called out his name in an attempt to rouse him from his sodden state. Moran responded by cursing and flailing at Tim with his arms. Tim ignored the gambler's demands to be allowed to sleep and doused him with a pitcher of water from a nearby stand.

Sobered and with his hair plastered down on his dripping forehead, the gambler stared at him, open-mouthed. 'Parker! What do you want?'

'Information, and pronto!' Tim snapped. 'Neilson was murdered tonight. Scalped same as the others.'

'No!' the gambler wailed, fear sobering him still more.

'Yes,' Tim snapped. 'It has to be Wolf. And you're the next name on the list. If you want to save your precious scalp, I suggest you tell me where Wolf usually hid out when he wanted to go undercover.'

'There were a lot of places,' the gambler moaned, holding his head in his hands. 'I'm finished! You'll never catch up with him.'

'Let me try,' Tim said. 'Give me a list of the probable places. And remember your life could depend on how well you remember.'

He could tell that Flash really tried. He

mentioned a half-dozen places, caves in the hills and some isolated cabins far distant from the town. Tim made a careful list of all of them and their locations. Then he left the unhappy gambler in a state of pure terror.

It was near dawn when Tim set out for the hills. He had the list with him, and detailed instructions how to find each of the five or six spots. With luck, he'd locate the half-breed in one of them. What happened after that was up to fate. But he had to stop Wolf's reign of terror. If he didn't, he was sure Susan would break under the burden of guilt she felt.

He'd never set out on a trail with more determination. And he had never met with such failure. The rosy dawn gave way to the bright sun of early morning, then the blazing rays and heat of midday. By late afternoon both he and the mare were weary and defeated. He paused at a water hole on his way to the sixth and last possible hide-out of the renegade Indian. So far he'd had no luck. Wolf had vanished into the wild country like a phantom.

The last isolated cabin proved to be as empty of life as the others. Tim saw how right Susan had been. He could search the hills and desert for months and never even glimpse the shadow of the half-breed. He had to find some other way, set a trap. With this thought to alleviate his weariness, he began the long ride back to Mad River.

Darkness had come, and the sky was plastered with stars, by the time he rode into the town. The cool darkness had revived both him and the mare. He made his way along the main street to the jailhouse, determined to put on the best possible face for Susan's benefit. He had to keep her spirits up.

He was about fifty yards from the jail when he became aware of a cluster of men and horses outside it. Fear for Susan shot through him as he nudged the weary mare forward at a faster gait. Reaching the fringe of the crowd, he dismounted and pushed his way through.

At the door, a cowpoke stood in his way. Tim demanded, 'What's going on here?'

'We're waiting for the sheriff,' the cowpoke said.

'I'm the deputy,' Tim said, indicating his badge. 'Where is she?'

'We don't know,' the cowpoke said. 'But she sure ain't here, and there's a dead man inside.'

Tim couldn't believe his ears. He moved on into the tiny office and down the short hall to the cells. There, sprawled in an open cell, was Flash Moran. And his head was a gory mess, for he'd been scalped like the others. Tim was sickened by the sight. While he'd been out in the hills searching for the half-breed, this weird drama had been taking place here. Flash Moran had come to see Susan for some reason, and Wolf must have followed him.

163

Keeping Susan prisoner, he'd scalped the gambler before her terrified eyes. Then he'd ridden off somewhere, taking her with him as a hostage.

The rough cattlemen were milling around him, going in and out of the cells, going where they had no right to be. But he couldn't muster his thoughts or command any proper authority for the moment. He stood there in the cell, which was lit by the flickering glow of a candle burning in a holder set into the wall of the corridor. His eyes blankly wandered along the scarred plaster wall.

Then he paused, and his body tensed. Quite by accident his eyes had caught the vague outlines of a word marked in the dust of the wall. In the twisting candle's flame, the wavering light had briefly illuminated the crude lettering. Tim took a deep breath and read the word which he prayed might have been put there by Susan as she crouched back, trembling, and watched the killer scalp Moran.

He turned and made his way out of the crowded jailhouse. In the street he asked for and was quickly given the loan of a fresh horse. Then he grimly set out from town again. He hoped he'd be in time to prevent another murder, maybe two!

For the word drawn in the dust of the cell wall had been 'castle'. It meant that Wolf was

164

taking Susan to the castle built on the desert's edge by Sam Smith. Tim wondered why he hadn't gone there before. It was the ideal hiding place for the half-breed. The Sioux looking after the old man would shelter Wolf. And hadn't Sam Smith gloomily predicted they would probably turn on him one day? Tim urged the horse on.

It was close to midnight when he got there. The great castle loomed ghostly and silent against the starry sky. Tim dismounted and went to the front entrance. The great oaken door was ajar, and there was no sign of the Sioux servants. He feared the worst and drew his Colt .44 out to have it ready for action. Very cautiously he entered the main hallway of the castle which the eccentric old man had erected in the barren spot.

Eerie silence and empty shadows greeted him everywhere in the high-ceilinged room. He moved on, his body slightly crouched, ready for action, the .44 drawn and his finger touching lightly on the trigger. Then he heard footsteps in the hallway above, racing footsteps.

Hurrying up the broad stairway, he went down the hallway, following the elusive footsteps. As he reached a second narrow flight of stairs, he heard an almost identical sound from above. Abandoning some of his caution, he rushed up the next flight and, reaching the head of the stairs, looked up and down the gloomy corridor. But he could see nothing.

'Drop your gun, Parker!' The words came in a rasping tone from the shadows. 'Drop it or I'll drill you!' There was no room for argument. Tim dropped his gun and turned around with a stunned expression on his handsome face.

'It's me, Sam,' he said. 'You don't have to be afraid. I've come to help you capture Wolf.'

'That's right generous of you,' Sam Smith said as he emerged from the shadows with his gun aimed at Tim. 'But the fact is: Wolf don't happen to be here.'

'He has to be. He took Susan with him.'

Sam Smith let out a weird cackle of laughter. 'That wasn't Wolf; it was me. I got the gal here. I figure she may come in handy later.'

And then it hit Tim with frightening impact. Sam Smith was his enemy. The crazy old prospector holding the gun on him was the one who'd done all the scalpings and led them on a wild chase. And it was he who now held Susan as hostage.

In a husky voice Tim asked, 'Why?'

The weird old man took a step nearer, his gun still pointed at Tim. A gloating expression crossed his wizened face. 'Everybody in Mad River tagged me as a crazy old man. But I was the brains behind it all. Trent and Neilson and the judge were just doing what I told them. The raids were organized here, and it was my Indians who led them, along with Wolf and a few others who'd do 'most anything for a bottle of whiskey.'

'You are responsible for all those scalpings?' Tim asked in a horrified fascination.

'Yep.' The little man nodded. 'I learned all about that when I spent a couple of years in the Sioux camps. Do it nice and neat, don't I? I had to rush Moran a little, since the gal was making such a fuss!'

'Why did you kill Moran?'

'He knew about me,' Sam Smith said calmly. 'He made the mistake of telling me and trying to make a deal. When he realized he was going to be next, he hit out for the jail to tell Susan. But I wasn't far behind him.'

'You're out of your mind,' Tim said, 'a crazy man.'

'That's what they've always called me,' Sam Smith cackled. 'But when I get rid of you and the gal, there won't be anyone left who knows. Nobody but my housetame Sioux, and they'll never talk. And when the railway comes, this crazy man will own the whole district. What do you say to that, Mr.. Parker?'

The old man's triumphant question was never answered. Or rather it was answered in

167

a way he didn't expect—by a bullet. It came from the other end of the landing. The shot was true. The old man looked surprised, dropped the gun he was holding and stumbled forward onto the carpet. There he lay very still. Tim swallowed hard and stared at the shadows where the bullet had come from. As he watched, a figure took shape. It was Wolf, the half-breed who'd dropped Sam Smith and saved his life.

Explanations came slowly. But by the time Tim found Susan, trussed up but safe in a basement room, he'd learned the whole story. The Sioux, who had long hated their master, had been giving Wolf shelter. And Wolf had been waiting for a chance to vindicate himself. Yet he'd dared not show himself in Mad River. In the end Sam Smith had played into his hands.

Susan was trembling as Tim pressed her to him in the dark room. He comforted her. 'Smith is dead. And your hunch about Wolf being innocent was right.'

'I know,' she said, pressing tightly against him. 'I can't believe it's over.'

'It is,' Tim said. 'And these last few hours have helped me make up my mind about a lot of things. I want to stay on in Mad River and marry you. I figure I may be able to talk myself into the job of sheriff. That is, if you'll trade in your silver star for a wedding ring.'

She looked up at him with loving eyes. 'Are

you sure you don't mind your youngsters having a touch of Sioux blood?'

'I wouldn't have it any other way,' he assured her, and sealed the bargain with a kiss.

Photoset, printed and bound in Great Britain by
REDWOOD BURN LIMITED, Trowbridge, Wiltshire

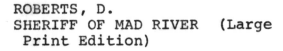